Mascot

There's a tough season ahead in the Sunday Junior League for Darton United when their coach, local soccer star Bryn Marsden, is transferred. Darton's captain, Damian Tennant, has to face up to a challenge to his leadership from within the team. Is he the right person for the job?

Also by Michael Hardcastle

FOOTBALL STORIES
Away From Home
Free Kick
Half A Team
Soccer Special
The Team That Wouldn't Give In
United!

MOTOCROSS STORIES
Fast From the Gate
The Green Machine
Roar to Victory
Tiger of the Track

RIDING STORIES
The Saturday Horse
The Switch Horse
Winning Rider

Caught Out (A Cricket Story)
Rival Games (An Athletics Story)
The Shooters (A Netball Story)

Michael Hardcastle regularly visits schools and libraries around the country. If you would like to meet him, please ask your teacher or librarian to write to the address below:

MAMMOTH Press Office
38 Hans Crescent
London SW1X 0LZ

MICHAEL HARDCASTLE

Mascot

MAMMOTH

First published in Great Britain 1987
by Methuen Children's Books Ltd
Magnet paperback edition published 1989
Published 1991 by Mammoth
an imprint of Mandarin Paperbacks
Michelin House, 81 Fulham Road, London SW3 6RB
Reprinted 1992

Mandarin is an imprint of the Octopus Publishing Group,
a division of Reed International Books Ltd

ISBN 0 7497 0901 4

A CIP catalogue record for this title
is available from the British Library

Printed in Great Britain
by Cox & Wyman Ltd, Reading, Berkshire

One

Damian Tennant replaced the telephone receiver with a sense of bewilderment.

'They're not going to believe this, they're definitely *not* going to believe it,' he said to himself, shaking his head. He was still standing in the hall, transfixed, when his mother came down the stairs, twirling her badminton racket and wearing an even shorter white dress than usual.

'Seen a ghost, darling?' she asked cheerfully, pausing to check her appearance in the full-length mirror on the wall beside the front door.

'Not exactly,' Damian told her. 'But just as unbelievable.'

'Must have something to do with football, then,' Mrs Tennant observed, with a lopsided grin. Damian knew she always put on that expression when she was mocking one of his obsessions.

'Of course it has!' he told her, a trifle irritatedly. 'What else is so important?'

'My badminton! And if I don't dash Jenny will be

looking for another partner. But you'd better tell me what's happened. Quickly, though.'

'Bryn Marsden's leaving City, that's what. Been transferred to Charlton. I don't know how we're going to manage without him. It's a total disaster.'

'But I thought City were having a good season, winning almost every match and –'

'I'm not talking about City,' Damian cut in. 'I mean *us*, Darton United. Bryn's still our coach, you know. Oh, and he's still our President.'

'Oh, but you'll manage to get somebody else, I expect,' Mrs Tennant said confidently. She was well aware that her son had a tendency to worry unnecessarily about his football life.

'I'm not sure about that,' Damian said doubtfully. 'It took us ages to find somebody like him in the first place. He made all the difference to our team. Without him we'd probably still be at the bottom of the Sunday League – or near the bottom, anyway.'

Sue Tennant scratched one slim, bare leg just above the knee and took another glance at her watch. 'Well, perhaps Bryn can suggest one of his team-mates as a replacement as a parting gesture to you.'

Damian gave her a calculating look. 'That's one of the unbelievable bits, Mum. He's already thought about a farewell present for me. He's fixed it for me to be the mascot for City's next home match. It's against Plymouth a week on Saturday.'

Mrs Tennant looked delighted. 'Well, that's marvellous, darling. Good for you. I know you'll really enjoy that. Surely that makes up for the disappointment over Bryn's leaving? So, look cheerful, stop being down in the dumps! Look, I just must fly. I – '

'There is something else,' Damian told her reflectively.

'Go on,' she said, trying not to let her exasperation get the upper hand.

'Well, the rest of the squad – the United squad, I mean – have been chosen as ball boys for the same match.'

'So what's wrong with that?' His mother was genuinely puzzled.

'They might be jealous because I've been singled out as mascot.'

'Oh, nonsense! You're the captain so you should get preferential treatment. That's only fair. They're bound to see that, Damian. I mean, you saved the whole team when things were really black for you last year – or last season, was it?'

'Last season. But Ian might not,' he told her flatly.

'Why on earth not?'

'Well, now he's fully fit again after his broken leg I think he wants to be captain again.'

'Has he said so?'

'Not exactly. But you see, Mum – '

'Darling, go I must! We can talk this over later – at supper time, if you like. It'll keep till then, won't it?'

'I suppose so. But can I ring the other players to give them the news? It's only fair to tell them as soon as possible.'

'All right,' agreed his mother, seizing her car keys from the wicker tray by the coat-stand. 'But keep the chat down, Damian. We can't afford another whopping phone bill like the last one. You and your vice-captain ought to share the information relay service between you, I reckon.'

Even when he'd seen his mother's silver saloon disappear from sight down the avenue, Damian hesitated over making the first call. He was thinking that he should speak to Alex Anson, United's vice-captain, first; and yet his instinct was to make contact with Ian Venn, his partner in midfield. The previous season, when United were in dire trouble at the bottom of the Redbourne Sunday League, Ian had become captain: but, as it turned out, only for a few minutes because in a training session his left leg had been smashed in a tackle by his team-mate, Paul Merchant. That was when Damian had taken over.

United had started the current season quite well and were in the top half of the table. They had a settled side, an inventive coach in Bryn Marsden, and most of the boys had a feeling they could even win a trophy before the season was over. For the first time in Damian's experience with the team, everything seemed to be in United's favour.

Ian had slotted back into the midfield as if he'd never been away and showed no ill-effects from his injury. So far he hadn't said a word (at least, not in Damian's hearing) about wanting to be captain again; he had simply followed Damian's leadership like everyone else. Ian didn't say much at any time but when he did open his mouth it was usually to say something sensible. In his conversation, as in his play on the field, he could be relied upon to make a worthwhile contribution. Nonetheless, Damian had a feeling that Ian would like to take over the team and run things his way.

Damian picked up the receiver, let his forefinger hover over the buttons, hesitated, bit his lower lip – and then plonked the phone down again. 'Go and see him,' he told himself. 'See how he takes things.' So, after checking that the cat was out of the house, he slammed the front door and set off up the avenue at a steady jog. It was only after he reached the junction with Sundial Hill that he remembered he ought to have brought an old tennis ball with him for dribbling and shooting practice. 'Whenever you're out, either on your own or in pairs, take a ball with you,' Bryn had advised. 'If you're on the move and you can train at the same time you're bound to improve your skills.'

Mrs Venn, who answered the ring on the side-door bell, seemed pleased to see him. 'Ian's in the sitting-room, watching some rubbish on television,' she announced, shaking her head sadly. 'I can't believe you've come to see the same programme, Damian. You're too intelligent for that.'

'Of course!' Damian grinned.

Ian managed to look apologetic as he lifted himself off the arm of a chair when Damian walked in with Mrs Venn peering over his shoulder. 'I sort of got hooked on this monster stuff when I was laid up with my broken leg,' he explained.

'Oh, you don't have to apologise to me, Ian,' Damian said in a tone of mock-superiority. Then, when he was sure that Mrs Venn was out of ear-shot, he added softly: 'I watch quite a lot of rubbish myself when nobody else is around to notice. Listen, I've just had some amazing news and I came round to tell you before anyone else.'

He studied Ian's face as he disclosed the details of Bryn Marsden's move to Charlton and the invitation to the United players to be the ball boys for the Plymouth match; but Ian's expression didn't alter much, although he kept tugging at a lock of his straw-coloured hair as if trying to make it still shorter. Damian recognised that as one of his regular habits. It was only when he mentioned being chosen as mascot that Ian displayed some emotion.

'You jammy devil!' he exclaimed. 'That's the one thing I've always wanted to be, ever since I went to see City play for the first time. It must be, well, fantastic to go out on to the pitch with the players and have the kick-around before the game begins. Oh, and you usually get the coin from the referee after they've tossed up – to keep, I mean. Sometimes it's a pound! Oh, the whole thing must be great.'

Damian was a little embarrassed by such fervour. 'I didn't know you felt so strongly about it,' he said quietly.

'I don't usually say how I feel about things, unless I really have to,' Ian replied in his more familiar cool manner.

Damian wandered across to a bookcase behind the television set and fiddled with the spine of a leather-bound volume. He didn't know whether he should say what was in his mind; but he wanted to be fair to a boy he thought of as a friend as well as a team-mate.

'In a way,' he said eventually. 'I suppose you ought to be the mascot. I mean, you would have been the captain if you hadn't broken your leg. I only got the job because of that, didn't I?'

'Yes,' was the blunt answer. 'So are you going to give the job up, then?'

Damian was taken aback by Ian's attitude but he responded immediately and instinctively. 'No, definitely not!'

'Well, that's it, then. You'll be the mascot and I won't. So I'll just be with the rest of the team, chucking the ball back when it goes out of play. Better than nothing, I suppose – and at least we'll get into the match free!'

'Er, Ian, what do you think we should do about finding a new coach?' asked Damian, anxious to change the subject.

'Have you asked Alex what he thinks?'

'You know I haven't! I just told you, I came round to give you all the news first.'

'Well, he's the vice-captain and I don't think he'll be very pleased with you if you don't consult him first. Alex likes to get involved in running things, you know. He often has good ideas. Alex is a bit of a thinker on the quiet.'

Damian had no doubt about that; he appreciated Alex's thoughtful contributions to team planning and the support he provided during matches if things were going against Darton United. Because Alex was the studious-looking type, and bird-watching was his chief hobby when not playing football, other boys tended to overlook the role he took in team affairs. In fact, Damian now recognised that he himself didn't always confer with Alex as often as perhaps he should. Ian's remark had made him feel more than a little guilty.

'Yeah, well I was going to see him after coming to you,' Damian said weakly.

'Got any other brilliant ideas?' Ian asked.

Damian was now distinctly disturbed by Ian's sarcastic tone. He hadn't imagined that Ian could feel so strongly about the captaincy. If this resentment continued, team morale would soon be affected.

'Well, I did ask you what you thought about getting a new coach – then I can tell Alex your views.'

Ian was now tapping his teeth with a pencil and seemed to be thinking very carefully what to reply. It was obvious to him that Damian was upset but Ian rarely allowed personal feelings to deflect him from getting what he wanted out of life. Now that he was fully fit again and, in his opinion, playing as well as ever, he believed strongly that he should be in charge of the team. On the other hand, he realised that Damian was popular with the majority of the United players and therefore they'd be unlikely to vote against him at any meeting. Ian guessed that the best way for him to regain the leadership would be to find some way of persuading Damian to resign the captaincy.

'It's my view that we don't need another coach,' he said positively. 'Bryn taught us a lot and I'm grateful for all he's done for the team. But I reckon we can get along fine without him or anyone else. I mean, the team's playing well. We don't want to risk somebody coming along and trying to change our tactics, our style. That would be – lunacy.'

'Yes, but – '

'Hang on! I hadn't finished. I was going to say that all we need now is a committee – say four of the players – to run the team and decide if we need to make any changes for any reason. Any reason at all.'

'A committee! Football teams aren't run by committees. That's crazy – '

'It isn't! My dad says all the best decisions are made by really good committees. And he should know. He sits on a few because he's got a top job in education.'

Damian was baffled. He was sure this wasn't a good idea at all and he couldn't think why Ian should be so enthusiastic about it; except that . . .

'I suppose you want to be on this committee, don't you?' he asked.

'Well, if you want me to be, yes, of course,' Ian replied without a second's hesitation. 'I'm also on a committee at my school so I know how they work. I think there should be four guys on our team committee – you, me, Alex and one other. If it were up to me I'd invite Jonathan McGuigan to join us. He's very keen on getting us up the League and improving our image. Jonathan's willing to help in any way. Look how he became our goalie when we needed one, even though he's really an outfield player.'

'I'd forgotten that,' Damian confessed. 'I just remember that Alex found him for us. They played in the same team at their school.'

'Jonathan really plays on the left side of midfield – like you,' Ian informed him. 'Anyway, what do you think about having him on our committee?'

Damian thought of saying that he hadn't exactly agreed that there should be a committee but he didn't want to risk upsetting Ian at this stage; in any case, if they didn't succeed in finding a new coach it might be a good move. At present all the responsibility for organising things was on the captain's shoulders; and, following Bryn Marsden's departure, his task would be harder still.

'I'll work on it,' Damian promised. 'Oh, and I'll see what Alex thinks. I'm going round to see him now with all the news. Then the three of us – oh, and Jonathan – can have a discussion after the match against Fyfield next Sunday. We'll have lots to talk about then, anyway.'

'Sure,' Ian agreed, accompanying Damian to the door.

Then, just as they were parting, Damian had a sudden thought. 'Hey, shouldn't we have somebody else on the committee to make it an odd number? You know, in case of a vote to decide anything that – '

'Oh no, I don't think that'll be necessary,' Ian cut in smoothly. 'I mean, we aren't likely to fall out over anything, are we?'

Two

The excitement in the Darton United dressing-room had nothing whatsoever to do with the match the team was about to play. Hardly anybody was even thinking about that: all the discussions were revolving around the news that the players were to act as ball boys at the Redbourne City v Plymouth Argyle match the following Saturday. Some, like Alex Anson and Jonathan McGuigan, had known about the invitation for several days, but this was the first time they'd been able to talk about it with the rest of the squad.

'Hey, I've just thought of something bad,' exclaimed Stevie Pailthorp, the speedy right-winger. He appeared quite crestfallen. 'We won't be able to wear our normal green shirts, will we, because Plymouth play in green? I mean, the referee will be worried about a colour clash, won't he?'

There was a momentary silence to greet the remark and then Billy Sandford said cuttingly: 'You nut, Stevie! Ball boys don't wear their own shirts. They're all in track suits. So – '

'But we haven't got track suits – not as a team, anyway,' Alex pointed out. 'The teams I've seen acting as ball boys at the City Ground have all been sponsored. You know, by a local garage or a supermarket or something. Maybe we should look for a sponsor quickly so that we can get track suits with our names on – oh, and theirs, too – for next Saturday.'

'That's good thinking, Alex,' Ian Venn told him. 'We should look into it right away.'

'I don't think there's going to be time to get that sort of thing fixed before next Saturday,' Damian pointed out as he pulled on his own No. 6 shirt and tucked it into his yellow shorts. 'Anyway, I expect City have some spare track suits, perhaps the ones the apprentices use. We can ask Bryn about that.'

'Bryn'll be too busy to think about us now,' Ian said. 'Anyway, he's already in London, isn't he? That's why he's not coming to our match today.'

'Er, yes,' Damian agreed. 'But his first match for Charlton is going to be next Sunday, so he's hoping to be at City's match with Plymouth – just as a spectator, of course. He's bound to want to see us at half-time and probably before the game begins as well.'

He could see that Ian wasn't convinced of Bryn Marsden's continuing interest in them, but he wasn't going to spend time arguing about that now. The vital thing was to concentrate on the preparations for their match against Fyfield Swifts; if they could defeat them then United would climb another rung of the Sunday League ladder to success. Bryn wasn't there to offer them any advice or to suggest changes of tactics if necessary during the course of the game. It was up to Damian himself to plan for everything as well as to lead the team both on and off the pitch. Although he had talked about this situation with the vice-captain, Alex hadn't offered to take on any of the responsibilities of running the team. He had given Damian the impression that his only real concern was his own form as one of the back-four players. Alex was two-footed but he tended to favour the right flank whereas Damian preferred him to stay in the middle of the defence.

'Listen, do you think we'll all get our pictures in the paper after Saturday?' Billy Sandford was asking everyone when Damian interrupted him by calling for silence.

'Look, I think we've got to forget about next Saturday and start to concentrate on today's game,' he said when he thought he had everyone's attention. 'If we don't get a good result today we won't be able to enjoy ourselves at the City Ground.'

'That's what you think!' Billy murmured, but loud enough for Damian to hear. He wanted to get his own back for being cut off. But this time nobody seemed to be listening to him.

'Fyfield are a pretty fair side and we won't be able to relax for a minute.' Damian carried on as if nobody had said a word. 'So I think we've got to attack right from the kick-off and put them under a lot of pressure. They've got a good home record so I expect they think visiting sides will be a bit nervous to start with. I mean, that usually happens.'

There he paused, not quite certain what to say next. Normally Bryn would have turned up by now and thrown in a few inspirational phrases to remember on the pitch. But Bryn wasn't here to inspire him or anyone else: and probably wouldn't be again. So Damian had to be coach as well as captain. He'd been looking at Stevie Pailthorp and now he remembered an idea he'd had.

'Stevie, you probably noticed as we came in how wide this pitch is. Well, that could help us if you make good use of your speed. I want you to stay out on the touch-line as much as possible. That'll drag their defence apart because somebody'll have to keep a watch on you. Then when you get the ball make for the corner flag – keep everything as wide as possible. OK?'

'And what do you want me to do when I get to the corner flag, then?' Stevie asked in a tone that just might have contained a hint of sarcasm.

Damian frowned. 'Well, what you usually do, of course: either send in a good cross or cut inside for a one-two with one of the other strikers. The point I'm making is that we want to keep their defence stretched. Right, anybody else got any questions?'

Deliberately he looked at each of his players. The only one not to meet his gaze was Ian, bouncing a spare ball near the entrance to the showers and seemingly counting each bounce.

'Any ideas, Ian?' he inquired.

Ian looked surprised and shook his head. 'No,

nothing.'

'Right,' Damian said positively. 'Let's go and get at 'em.'

That didn't sound right, coming from him, and he knew it. The phrase was what Bryn Marsden called their battle cry: he'd coined it and uttered it before the start of every match and the players reacted to it eagerly. Damian recognised that all he himself had done was remind them of Bryn's absence. That wasn't helpful at all. In future, he'd have to come up with a battle cry of his own.

As soon as he saw the assembled Fyfield team Damian wished, for the umpteenth time, that he was at least a couple of inches taller. Although he had strong thigh and calf muscles and could jump to a good height, there were times when he felt much too short: and this was one of them. By comparison with United, the Fyfield players, in their blue-and-white hooped shirts, seemed enormous. All Damian could hope was that their play wasn't as powerful as their appearance. Because Fyfield had been relegated at the end of the previous season, Darton hadn't encountered them before (Darton never having played in a higher division of the Redbourne Sunday League).

The Swifts were determined to get promotion at the earliest opportunity and they had plenty of vocal support from enthusiastic parents and other supporters; in contrast, United hadn't a single person off the pitch to shout for them. Damian's mother had promised many times to turn up to an away match but she hadn't made it yet and on this Sunday morning she was playing in what she told her only son was another 'absolutely vital' badminton game. Perhaps, Damian reflected, if he went to watch her in action her conscience would compel her to return the compliment.

Light rain was falling as the match began and the Swifts immediately lived up to their name by darting all over the place, unpredictably and at rare speed; with the ball skidding off the wet long grass, control wasn't easy and United's defence committed several uncharacteristic errors in the opening minutes. It was only by good luck and the length of Jonathan's fingers that Fyfield didn't score three times in that period. Damian, dropping back to help his beleaguered back-four, praised Jonathan and patted him on the back as they waited for a corner kick to be taken. Fyfield's tallest player, their centre-back, got in a header which skimmed only just over the bar with, this time, Jonathan ill-positioned to cope with it had the ball been on target.

'You ought to have been marking their centre-back, you're almost his height,' Damian murmured to Neil Dallimore, United's main striker, when they met moments later in midfield. 'We can't afford to let them get in free headers from set-pieces.'

'Somebody has to stay up front in case of a breakaway,' Neil muttered. 'I mean, I am here to score goals, you know.'

There was no time to say anything further. Damian had to move quickly to pick up a loose ball and fire it at

Ian Venn.

For once Ian wasn't paying attention. When he failed to trap the ball properly he turned slowly to try to retrieve it and was far too late. Fyfield's left-winger had already snapped it up and, urged on by the baying home crowd, was making rapid progress down the flank.

'Wake up, Ian!' Damian yelled in exasperation as he chased back towards his own penalty area to provide additional cover.

Ian shot him a fierce and surprised look but didn't retaliate. He knew he'd been at fault and he hated to make mistakes. All the same, he didn't care to have those mistakes pointed out in public. Rapidly he set off in pursuit of the opponent who'd taken the ball off him. By now, however, the winger had cut inside and then, after selling a dummy to Alex Anson, he drove the ball all along the ground towards the far side of the penalty area. There to meet it was the Swifts' smallest and nippiest attacker. Cleverly he stopped the ball, dragged it back under his foot as Paul Merchant tried to dispossess him, jinked sideways and then, with splendid accuracy, drove his shot beyond Jonathan's despairing reach into the far corner of the net.

'Oh, great goal, great goal!' yelled the boy's father, one of the most vociferous of the spectators. He firmly believed that his son would play for Arsenal (and probably England) one day and his only regret was that no scout from Highbury was present to see such clinical finishing.

Damian didn't know what to say as Jonathan

retrieved the ball. The goalkeeper hadn't really been at fault and although he thought that Paul should have tackled his opponent sooner he wasn't to blame, either. The goal chance had actually stemmed from Ian's failure to take a pass, but no good would come from harping on that: he'd already made his view plain on that point.

Fyfield hadn't been lacking in confidence before that goal, but now they set about Darton United as if they believed they could slaughter them. For the next ten minutes or so the green-shirted visitors were penned in their own half of the field – and mostly in and around the penalty area. Every booted clearance from there was almost always promptly returned by Fyfield's sweeper, now operating just inside United's half. To his ill-concealed disapproval, Neil Dallimore had been ordered to help the defenders and it was his clumsiness which very nearly cost Darton a second goal: a goal that, Damian believed, would have killed off their hopes of getting any points out of the game.

The gangling striker had improved his play greatly since the end of the previous season, but he was still liable to make the most ridiculous mistakes in any quite ordinary situation. Alex had once remarked that Neil was simply 'disaster-prone' and that was a fair description. If anyone was going to fall over because of standing on the ball instead of trapping it, that player was Neil Dalli-a-lot, to use the nickname several of his team-mates favoured. Now, on the edge of the United box, he intercepted a pass from a Fyfield forward, failed to control the ball, lost it to another player and, in his desperation to regain it, lunged at his opponent and knocked him to the ground.

It was clearly a foul and, in spite of Neil's protests that it was a fair tackle, the referee pointed to a mark barely inches outside the penalty area. Hastily Damian organised a defensive wall. Neil was ordered to station himself right in the middle of it so that whoever took the free kick would have difficulty in chipping the ball over him. Jonathan, dancing up and down on his line, was pleading for a clear view of the kicker.

Fyfield summoned up one of their midfielders, who could strike the ball with the force of a cannon. Clearly the team didn't believe in subtlety where the taking of free kicks was concerned. The ball was blasted at the wall, causing Paul Merchant to double up with the agony of taking the impact in the midriff, and then bounced invitingly for an attacker to try a lob into the top corner of the net. Although he saw the shot coming only at the last second, Jonathan's reach was enough for him to palm the ball round the post.

The corner kick had to be delayed, however, for Paul to receive prolonged treatment from Fyfield's coach. It was one of Damian's perpetual worries that United lacked a regular supporter who possessed medical knowledge or healing powers or both. If one of their players was injured then they invariably had to rely on the opposition or casual spectators for help. Paul was really only severely winded but he was giving the impression that he felt he should have been rushed to hospital for emergency treatment.

'Come on, Paul, you'll live,' Damian told him, a trifle unsympathetically. 'You should learn to protect yourself better at free kicks.'

Fyfield, having grown impatient at the delay, wasted the kick when it was taken and Alex was thankful to hoof the ball to the half-way line. It was soon back in United territory again, however, and the siege was only relieved when Damian himself collected the ball and began a mazy dribble that took him out to the right wing; there he dummied to pass to Stevie and made further progress before hitting a beautifully-judged long pass to Neil Dallimore. For once Neil kept his feet and control of the ball; his only mistake was to hit his shot far too soon because he could have taken the ball another few yards before shooting. But at least United had the satisfaction of launching an attack on the Swifts' goal.

A couple of minutes later Damian was wondering how soon the referee would blow for half-time. He, for one, would be glad of a rest. Fyfield, too, seemed conscious of the time factor and were pressing hard for a second goal that would surely demoralise the opposition. The ball was switched to Tim, their goal-scorer, and this time he was intent on a solo run. Paul Merchant was his nearest opponent but he made no attempt to go in for a tackle. He was backing off, backing off, all the way into the penalty area. Jonathan, too, took no purposeful action – until it was too late.

Tim, with the goal now in his sights, suddenly and

dramatically accelerated. Because he'd been retreating at a slowish pace Paul couldn't react quickly enough and he simply fell over when he tried to change direction. Jonathan belatedly decided to come off his line to narrow the angle for the shot; but by then the astute Tim had picked his spot and was slotting the ball past the goalkeeper and into the vacant net.

'What do you think you were doing?' Damian stormed at Paul. 'Why didn't you get in there and tackle him?'

For a moment or two Paul made no reply at all. His round face was pink with embarrassment. 'Well, I didn't want to go in hard and risk getting hurt again,' he admitted.

Damian was staggered. 'What d'you mean?' he demanded.

Paul looked unhappier still, if that were possible. 'Well, you see, Damian, I was thinking about – about next Saturday. I don't want to miss being one of the ball boys. That'd be – well, a disaster.'

This time Damian was speechless. He would never have believed that a player would calculate his chances of being injured before going in to tackle an opponent when his team was in danger of conceding a goal. He turned and trudged back to the centre for the resumption.

At half-time, however, he had to find something to say: something to encourage the team to keep trying for victory and something about tactics for the second half. A pep talk was expected of him as it would be of any coach or manager in similar circumstances. If he, as the captain, appeared downhearted then the team couldn't be expected to fight for survival.

'They're not as good as they think they are, you know,' he said, thinking aloud between mouthfuls of banana, his favourite food on match day. 'We're just letting 'em over-run us, we're not hitting back. We've got to believe in ourselves.'

He knew that Bryn was a great believer in believing in yourself and that he'd probably expressed the same thought dozens of times; but that didn't matter. The only important thing was to make his team-mates think about the match and their own game.

Ian, now bouncing a spare ball from one forearm to the other in a new style of juggling, waited for the pause and then said: 'Well, you know what's wrong, don't you, skipper?'

Damian, ignoring the deliberate emphasis on the word skipper, asked what Ian had in mind.

'More pace down the middle, that's what's lacking,' Ian told them. 'If we don't get some real attacks in then we can't hope to score, can we?'

'And where are we going to get that from?' Damian wanted to know.

'Well, for a start I think Stevie should move inside, up alongside Neil,' suggested Ian. 'We're too spread out to make any worthwhile attacks.'

'Yeah, I agree,' Stevie contributed. 'This pitch is a bit too wide. When I put a cross in there's nobody there for it if it drops a bit short.'

Damian could have pointed out that this was because Stevie wasn't putting enough beef into his centres but he decided that remark mightn't be helpful. Stevie was the sort of player who responded to praise, not adverse criticism. Still, Ian's idea had some merit and Damian was perfectly willing to try it. He asked if anyone else had suggestions and, as he did so, he looked at Alex. But neither the vice-captain nor anyone else offered a single thought.

'OK,' he announced, 'we'll do that. Stevie you can move inside and combine with Neil. But don't get in each other's way!'

Ian, who had begun bouncing the ball on his right instep, grinned his approval and exchanged glances with Alex, which was something Damian didn't notice.

The rain was much heavier when play resumed so that the surface was becoming very slippery. Yet, to his team-mates' surprise, Neil displayed exceptional control after picking up a loose ball on the perimeter of the centre circle. Rounding Fyfield's centre-back with ease, he set off on a direct run to the penalty area with Stevie in close support and Ian just behind them. Another defender slipped out of contention after missing an attempt at a sliding tackle and Neil, following an exchange of passes with Stevie, had a clear sight of goal. His fierce drive was only parried by the goalkeeper whose reflexes were slow after being out of action for so long. Neil was unable to reach the rebound but Ian, following up, very coolly slammed the ball into the back of the net and then spun away, both arms aloft to signal his delight at scoring his first goal of the season.

'Hey, terrific goal!' yelled Damian, running across to congratulate the scorer. 'And well done, Neil. That was a great run of yours.'

Ian exchanged a cool shake of the hand with his captain and didn't say anything although he naturally looked well pleased with himself. Neil, inevitably, was telling team-mates, really, the goal ought to be credited to him because he'd done everything except put the ball in the net after hitting 'the hottest shot that goalie's ever had to handle'. Damian didn't mind who scored just so long as United were back in the game.

Surprisingly, Fyfield seemed to wilt instead of redoubling their efforts to restore their two-goal lead. Most of the players had written off Darton as no-hopers and now they couldn't immediately cope with the reality of United's skilful and successful counter-attack. They tended to rely on their band of adult supporters to encourage them instead of taking their lead from their captain; and now those adults were shouting conflicting advice. Some wanted the Swifts to 'close the game down and shut Darton out'; others urged 'attack, attack, attack and get another goal. A one-goal lead is never enough!'

In spite of their own renewed zeal and an abundance of attacking opportunities, United were finding it impossible to get the equalizer. More than once Neil and Stevie actually got in each other's way and good chances in front of goal were squandered. Ian, now that he had the taste for scoring, was pressing further and further forward. Nonetheless, the Swifts somehow managed to contain United's attack. Damian sensed that it would be a good idea to tell Stevie to exploit the width of the pitch again to pull Fyfield's defence apart. But if he did that Ian would probably regard the manoeuvre as treachery. What they lacked most of all was a left-winger with pace and penetration; but then that had always been so since Darton United was formed.

'Billy, keep out on the left touch-line as much as you can when we're going forward,' Damian instructed Sandford, who'd been having a fairly aimless time in the middle of the pitch. 'We've just got to change the point of attack.'

That was the sort of ploy that Bryn Marsden would use, Damian was convinced. But for him it back-fired almost at once. For, when Ian swept the ball out to the left flank Billy failed to control it with his left foot and, in the most obvious and painful fashion, he used his right foot to gain possession and then try and take on an opponent. With contemptuous ease the Fyfield player dispossessed him, leaving a dejected Billy sprawled on the grass. Billy, whose father had once been Darton's manager, didn't have much fight in him and he was inclined to sulk if things went badly wrong for him.

Gradually Fyfield had recovered their composure. They had repelled all the Darton raids, such as they were, and their own attack was beginning to function again. Best of all, there was no more helpful advice being offered from the touchlines. Their supporters restricted themselves to handing out praise when it was deserved. The Swifts were confident again of improving their promotion prospects. Then, with only three minutes of the match remaining, they had no doubt at all of a comfortable victory that would even improve their goal difference.

Because the Swifts' attacks had been so rare in the second half, Jonathan McGuigan had taken to straying further and further from his line as he tried to urge his team-mates to keep going forward. So he was ill-positioned when Tim received a speculative long pass out on the right wing where no one was marking him. Tim, noting the goalkeeper's wanderlust, took only a couple of steps before, with excellent aim, hitting the ball as hard and high as he could in the direction of the yawning net.

Jonathan was slow in seeing the danger. But even if he'd moved immediately, and at top speed, there was no hope of his getting back to the goal-line before the ball crossed it. Tim had completed his hat-trick with the most satisfying of his goals and, at the same time, sealed the Swifts' success. He thoroughly deserved the heaped congratulations of his team-mates and their enchanted supporters.

'What were you thinking about?' Damian asked his goalkeeper, more in dismay than in anger, as the teams left the field after the final whistle. 'You just about gave 'em that last goal.'

'I never expected him to shoot from there,' was

Jonathan's only reply.

'You know, we definitely ought to have won that match – or at least grabbed a draw,' Damian said to Ian Venn as they arrived at the entrance to the dressing-room together. 'We ought to have *built* on your goal. Instead . . .'

'We would have done if we'd had some strength and pace to help the attack down the left,' Ian replied. 'That's the sort of player we're missing.'

'Well, we've no hope of getting one,' Damian responded gloomily.

'Oh, I think we have,' Ian said quite chirpily. 'In fact,

I'm sure of it.'

Damian stood with his hands on his hips and stared at him. 'What have you got in mind?'

Ian grinned. 'Tell you at our first committee meeting. That's where we ought to have a proper discussion of tactics, isn't it?'

Three

It had always been Damian's dream to stroll through the players' entrance at Redbourne City's ground. He had imagined driving his luxurious sports car into the reserved space with his name on it in the private car park under the North Stand, and then receiving a salute and a friendly welcome from the official on duty just inside that desirable entrance. Probably he'd be asked to sign a few autographs for patiently-waiting youngsters and, of course, he would do so with a flourish and a word of encouragement for the autograph-seekers' own sporting careers. He'd smile his appreciation when they gushed 'Thanks a *lot*, Damian'. Somehow it wouldn't sound at all right if they addressed him as Mr Tennant.

Now, as he approached the huge grandstand after dropping off the bus in City Road, he wondered what sort of reception he'd receive. Already scatterings of spectators had arrived for the Second Division match and some were standing around in groups, waiting to see something worth seeing and Damian had to ask some older teenagers to move aside so that he could reach the players' entrance. He was relieved that none of them made any rude comments.

'Oh, you'll be one of the ball boys, I take it,' was the greeting he received from the dark-suited figure standing just inside the doorway.

'Well, actually, I'm the mascot,' Damian explained. He didn't know who this man was but he'd half-expected to be met by City's manager, Alistair McAndrew (or MacAndy as Bryn Marsden always called him when he talked to the boys at coaching sessions).

'Oh, that's even better, isn't it?' said the club official. 'That makes you a VIP for the day.'

'Pardon?'

'A Very Important Person – which of course you are anyway, I expect. Now, if you come through here and then go down that corridor to the second door on the right, you should find Ricky Bennett in his office. He's our Promotions Manager, as I expect you know and he'll look after you.'

'Thanks very much,' said Damian, setting off.

'Oh, by the way, I hope you bring us some luck, son,' the man called after him. 'Mascots are supposed to be lucky, you know.'

Damian had never met Ricky Bennett but he knew a good deal about him for the Promotions Manager had once been City's most prolific goal-scorer until his career was ended by a serious ankle injury which caused him to hobble even now. The door was wide open and

Ricky was speaking on the telephone; but he was alert to Damian's arrival and beckoned him in.

'Well, son, nice to see you,' he said when at last he put the phone down. He held out his hand for a firm and welcoming shake: 'You must be Damian. Heard a lot about you from Bryn. Says that your team is going places. Well, today they've come to the *right* place! I'm sure you're going to see a great match and you're going to help us win it. I mean, that's what you're here for, son, isn't it?'

Damian, finding it easy to respond to Ricky's warmth and enthusiasm, agreed that it was. Then he listened carefully as he was told exactly what was going to happen to him during the course of the afternoon, though more than once Ricky had to break off to take another telephone call or have a brief word with a visitor.

He was disappointed that he wasn't going to be allowed to change in City's dressing-room with the players for that is what he'd wanted more than anything; he would have felt part of the team. But he didn't let that disappointment show as Ricky reached into a cupboard and then handed him the strip normally worn by the mascot; it was, of course, identical to that worn by the City players: scarlet shirt and shorts and white-banded black socks. In fact, Damian had once been presented with a City shirt by Bryn Marsden and he wished now that he'd brought it with him to wear on this momentous occasion. But perhaps his club would think that was showing-off.

'Right, I'll take you along to the kit room where the ball boys always change and then when you're ready you can return to my office and I'll introduce you to the players just before they go out on to the pitch,' Ricky said, leading him down the endless-seeming corridor that ran almost the length of the grandstand. 'You'll be able to wave to your mum and dad from the pitch as well as join in the kick-about. Oh yes, and you'll get your photo taken. We'll give you a big blown-up print for your bedroom wall as a souvenir. It'll help you to remember the day.'

'I don't think I'll ever forget it as long as I live,' Damian said feelingly.

Several of his United team-mates had already arrived and were changing into club track suits when Ricky and Damian reached the narrow, triangular-shaped room hidden under the main concrete stairway at the far end of the stand. Because he was putting on a team shirt and shorts instead of the same outfit as everyone else, he soon felt on his own. Alex and Ian were deep in conversation and it was clear to Damian that they wouldn't welcome an interruption. Some of the others were chattering excitedly about the prospect of getting autographs or being spotted by League scouts as prospects for the future.

'Anyone seen Bryn?' Damian inquired generally, more in the hope of joining in a conversation than in getting information.

'I should have thought you'd see him before any of us,' replied Billy, 'seeing as you're mixing with the top people. We're just the slaves, you know, kept out of sight at the bottom of the ship.'

That provoked a laugh, much to Billy's delight because he wasn't renowned for possessing a sense of humour. So he immediately tried to crack a few more jokes and that made Damian feel completely excluded.

'See you,' he called out as he left the kit room but he didn't hear anyone respond.

He cheered up when Ricky, in a change of plan, took him along to the home team dressing-room a minute or so before the players were due on the pitch. Alistair McAndrew, who'd just delivered his pep talk, came across to present him with a City pennant and most of the players made a point of shaking his hand. Damian didn't have time to catch more than a glimpse of the famous deep bath which could take all the team and more. Moments later the referee looked in, exchanged quips with Mr McAndrew and said it was time they were all out in the sunshine to entertain the millions who'd come to see them.

'You go first, Damian – let the crowd see our latest record signing,' City's skipper told him cheerfully. Damian, grateful that his name had been remembered, was surprised to note that the player didn't appear to be feeling any tension at all. Yet Damian himself always felt nervous when he was about to lead United into a match.

The sun really was shining very brightly now and the roar that greeted the home side as they emerged from the narrow tunnel was much louder than Damian had expected. He very nearly dropped the spare ball he was carrying – that would have looked terrible.

As soon as he was on the hallowed pitch he drop-kicked the ball and then chased after it into the penalty area where City's goalkeeper and one of the full-backs fielded the shots that rained in on them during the shoot-in. Damian was presented with one or two good shooting chances and with the second of them he succeeded in putting the ball into the net, hitting it hard and low with his left foot. That provoked a small outburst of cheering and whistles from spectators behind the goal and Damian acknowledged it with a nonchalant wave.

He was so absorbed in the kick-about that he almost missed hearing his own name over the loud-speaker system but, after listing the Redbourne and Plymouth teams and the match officials, the announcer added: 'And today's mascot is Damian Tennant, who captains Darton United in the Junior Sunday League. Damian's team-mates, the other United players, are today's ball boys, so our sincere thanks to Darton United for their support.'

Damian wondered what his parents were thinking about all this. They, too, had been invited to the match and provided with seats in the main stand, close to the directors' box, where Damian would join them once the game started. He would have preferred to be a ball boy, too, but Ricky Bennett said that it was traditional for the mascot to be with his folks in the stand; and Damian felt it wouldn't be polite to try and argue against that.

The match had attracted a good crowd and it was quite impossible for him to pick out his parents from the pitch but he knew they'd be watching and so he gave another wave in that direction. He'd always imagined it would be marvellous to step on to City's pitch before a big match and so it was; now he decided it was the greatest thrill of his life. There could hardly be a greater one until the day he signed for City as a full-time professional player.

'Right, son, let's go and do the toss-up,' City's skipper called to him and they made their way to the centre circle where everybody shook hands with everyone else. An awful lot of time was taken up with hand-shaking, which seemed quite pointless to Damian.

'You can call if you like, Damian,' the skipper told him as the referee prepared to spin the coin.

That was totally unexpected and, suddenly, it seemed to Damian to be an awesome responsibility. Suppose he called wrong and . . . 'Heads,' he said firmly, shutting unwelcome thoughts out of his mind.

They all had to move as the ten-penny piece bounced down and then rolled so far it almost went out of the centre circle; but when they all stooped they discovered that City's mascot had made the right choice.

'Fine, we'll play towards the city end,' the skipper declared and then turned to grin at Damian. 'You seem to have got us off to a good start, Damian. Hope you enjoy the match. Nice meeting you.'

'Here you are, son, that's for you to keep,' said the

referee, handing Damian the coin and accompanying it with the inevitable handshake.

'Thanks a lot,' Damian replied and then turned to make his way off the pitch.

As he neared the touch-line he saw that Ian Venn had stationed himself as close to the managers' dug-out as possible as if hoping to pick up some useful advice.

'Hey, I told you you'd get the money,' he called to Damian. 'Going to buy us all a Coke after the match?'

'I don't think ten-pence will exactly run to that,' Damian told him before he entered the tunnel that would take him back under the main stand.

By now, of course, the place was practically deserted and Damian experienced a sense of isolation as he changed back to his ordinary clothes in the odd-shaped kit-room. More fiercely than ever, he wished they'd allowed him to be one of the ball boys; he thought he'd have sacrificed the glory of being the mascot for the chance to stay close to the pitch. Instead, he made his way up the stairs to the seats where his parents were watching the match with every sign of interest.

'You looked really good out there, just as if you belonged on the pitch,' his mother greeted him. 'You seemed to be part of the team.'

'I think I'm a bit on the short side for that,' Damian remarked wryly.

'You won't always be!' his mother assured him, squeezing his arm. 'Honestly, we feel very proud of you.'

Damian, after glancing quickly at the pitch to see

how City were getting on, switched his attention to the directors' box. There he hoped to see Bryn Marsden, perhaps sitting beside the Club's chairman as a farewell gesture. But there was no sign at all of Darton United's President and honorary coach. Perhaps, after all, he'd been detained in London; at that moment he might even be training with Charlton and getting to know his new team-mates before playing his first match the following day.

'I think your lot have got a fight on their hands this afternoon,' said his father, cutting into Damian's thoughts.

'Oh, they're a bit like us, they don't always make a brilliant start,' Damian replied. To Damian's abiding horror, his father actually preferred rugby, both to watch and to play. He was always inclined to make disparaging remarks about soccer when he was sure Damian was listening.

However, it was true. City were pinned in their own half by the fast-moving, inventive Plymouth side which kept up the pressure with considerable skill. The only surprise to date was that the green-shirted Devon side hadn't scored a goal to underline their superiority. Even when City managed a breakaway movement Argyle's sweeper, a Danish international, was always on hand to make a telling interception. Yet, at half-time, there was still no score.

'I suppose you're off to join your mates for a free feast,' said Damian's father, offering his wife a toffee.

'Well, nothing was said about that,' Damian

admitted rather sorrowfully. 'Ricky Bennett told me to take the kit back to his office and that's what I did. I mean, I've no idea where our team's gone. Probably they're just in the kit-room, waiting for the second half.'

'Oh, well, you'd better have a toffee, too!'

Damian chewed away and thought that being the mascot wasn't such a wonderful thing after all. It was all over so quickly and he didn't have much to show for it, apart from the Redbourne City pennant. No one had even taken his photograph with the two captains and the referee, something he'd seen happen at a televised match. Worst of all, he hadn't seen Bryn and he was separated from his team-mates. To avoid having to make any further conversation he studied the match programme with unusual intensity. Then he discovered his own name in it, along with a reference to the fact that he captained Darton United, and immediately he felt quite cheerful again. He casually pointed it out to his mother.

'Oh, I know,' she said, 'because I've read your dad's programme. But we didn't tell you because we wanted you to find out for yourself.'

The good news came abruptly to an end just two minutes after the second half began when Plymouth scored the goal their dominant play deserved: a diving, almost horizontal, header from an unexpectedly early cross by their right winger. Damian groaned aloud but made a mental note to tell Stevie Pailthorp to hit some low crosses from time to time.

Although he kept an eye on the directors' box in case Bryn turned up, Damian began to watch the ball boys in action. In fact, they rarely had anything to do because when the ball went out of play it was usually a player who retrieved it (or a spectator in the crowd if it went as far as that). So perhaps he wasn't missing much after all by sitting in the stand, he consoled himself.

'Come on, City!' he urged under his breath. 'Everybody'll think I let you down if you lose. I'll be the *unlucky* mascot.'

Five minutes of the match remained when, in trying to hook the ball clear of an opponent, a Plymouth defender sliced it out of play and then fell as he tried to recover his balance. As the ball flashed over the touch-line Ian caught it at full stretch and, without a moment's hesitation, lobbed it straight to a City player who was well-positioned to take a throw-in. He accepted it gratefully, threw it to a team-mate who, taking advantage of the absence of cover around the Plymouth penalty area, hit a high cross to the far side of the box.

The timing of that centre, as it turned out, was superb. As if in anticipation of receiving the ball, City's leading striker had begun to race towards the penalty area as the throw-in was taken. Now, right on cue, he arrived on the ideal spot to rise above his solitary opponent and direct a powerful header into the top right-hand corner of the net for City's equalizer.

Damian was on his feet an instant before the spectacular goal was scored, eager to applaud the movement, and Ian's quick thinking, which had led to it. He had sensed that the ball was going to finish up in the net. His only regret was that it wasn't Bryn Marsden who'd applied the finishing touch.

'Well, that was worth waiting for, I must say,' Mr Tennant commented, much to his son's surprise. 'I suppose you'll be happy for the rest of the week after that, will you?'

'Happier,' was all Damian would concede. 'I mean, we haven't won, have we? Just like Darton United, City need to win every match they can if they're going to get anywhere in the League.'

But City couldn't manage the winner although in the final moments of the match Plymouth were defending desperately. His parents assured Damian they'd thoroughly enjoyed the match in addition to seeing him on the pitch as the mascot.

'You going to catch up with your pals now, then?' his father inquired. 'You'll all have a lot to talk about.'

'Well, I don't know,' Damian said doubtfully. 'I mean, nothing was fixed about after the match and – '

'Oh, go on! You might have a chance of another word with the players. No point in missing out on things if you can join in.'

So, grateful for the insistence, Damian pushed his way through the crowd leaving their seats and then dashed down the wide stairway to the kit-room. And the first person he saw there, just inside the doorway and holding a gift-wrapped package in his hands, was Bryn Marsden. The rest of the United players, some of them already changed out of their track suits, were all looking at the coach expectantly.

'Ah hello, Damian,' Bryn greeted him with a wide smile. 'I was wondering what had happened to you. I mean, I can't open my present without the captain being here, can I? Or a parting gift I'd better call it, hadn't I?'

'Er, um, yes, I suppose so,' Damian stammered, baffled by what was going on. He tried to catch Alex's or Ian's eye but both were staring intently at Bryn.

'Well, how about that! A wallet – and in red leather, too,' he exclaimed, plainly delighted, when he'd torn away the wrapping. 'Just what I need. Honestly, boys, it's really very kind of you to give me this but you shouldn't have spent your hard-earned pocket money on me.'

'We thought you'd need another wallet now you've joined a London club and you'll get lots and lots of money,' Jonathan joked.

'I don't know so much about that! Anyway, it costs about five times as much to live in London as it does in Redbourne so I'll probably be even worse off there. One thing's for sure, though: I'll miss Darton United. So you've got to promise to keep me up-to-date with results. OK?'

'Oh, we'll do that, Bryn,' Ian promised before anyone else could say a word. 'We can send you a report on every match and the League table from the local paper if you like.'

'Fine, fine. Oh, and Ian, that was a really smart bit of

work of yours when you caught that ball and gave it to Charlie Miller for the quick throw-in. I reckon that was why we scored! Really good work, son.'

'Yes, I thought so, too, Ian. I had a very good view from the stand and *everybody* thought it was terrific,' Damian added, thinking it was about time he said something.

'Well, boys, I'm afraid I've got to say cheerio for now. Got to have a word with some of my mates – oh, and Ally MacAndy as well, of course. Got to keep in with your old boss, you know. Never know when you might need him again!'

But, before he actually hurried away, Bryn made a point of shaking each boy by the hand and wishing him well in the future. Damian was the one he reached last and for him he had a slap on the back, too.

'Well, son, I hope you enjoyed being mascot – you looked good out there, I must say. I was a bit late getting here so I sat at the back of the stand, otherwise I'd have come down to meet you. Anyway, if you keep leading United the way you have been doing, things can't go far wrong. So all the best, Damian.'

'All the best to you, Bryn – and thanks again for everything you've done for us,' Damian told him fervently. 'And you'll still be our President, you know.'

As soon as Bryn was out of earshot, Damian turned to Ian and demanded to know why he hadn't been told about the plan to make a presentation to their departing coach. After all, he was the captain and it was his job to hand over a gift like that. It was obvious to everyone that he was angry at not being involved.

'Well, it was just a spur-of-the-moment idea yesterday and you weren't around when Jonathan and I discussed it,' Ian replied calmly. 'We paid for it out of our own money but the rest of the team have all said they'll chip in their share. It's 60p each if you want to join in, Damian. But you can give us the money later if you haven't got it on you.'

Damian swallowed his wrath. There was no point in losing his temper, especially over something he approved of. He dug into his pocket for his contribution.

'But you could have told me in advance,' he pointed out, handing over the money. 'I mean, I saw you all in here before the game began.'

'Well, I just forgot,' admitted Ian, pulling on his favourite red-and-blue sweater. 'Anyway, we didn't know if you were coming back here, did we? You were off up in the stand doing your own thing. You weren't with the rest of us and *involved* in the match, were you?'

'I *wanted* to be! But the club fixed it that way, saying I should sit in the stand with my parents.'

'Yeah, well, it doesn't matter now, does it?' said Ian, heading for the exit. 'See you at the committee meeting on Tuesday. There'll be plenty to talk about then. Come on, Jonathan, let's get back to my place and play some pool.'

As Damian set off on his own journey home, a few minutes later, he began to worry about the Tuesday meeting. He sensed that his leadership of Darton United was now under threat.

Four

Damian was demolishing a doughnut when Ian Venn walked in to the Canary Café with Jonathan McGuigan. He had known they would arrive together because it was obvious that their friendship was growing all the time. Yet, originally, Jonathan had been Alex's friend and he'd been introduced to the United team when Ian was out of it. Lately Damian had been wishing that he had a close friend in the side, but none of his team-mates went to his school; so he had very little contact with them except on match days.

'I'm going to have a slice of fly cemetery,' Jonathan announced loudly. 'It's the best food there is.'

None of the other customers appeared to take any notice of this peculiar taste, rather to Jonathan's disappointment. Like many goalkeepers, he was always happy to show off when he was assured of an audience.

Ian, shrugging his shoulders resignedly at Damian, accompanied Jonathan to the counter and there took some time in choosing what he wanted; eventually he settled for a large slice of chocolate cake displayed in a bell-shaped glass case beside the tea urn. The Canary Café had built its reputation with the town's afternoon tea-takers on its distinctly old-fashioned style. Its proprietor even addressed his adolescent customers (who were in the majority at this time of day) as 'Young sir' or 'Young lady.' His courtesy was so plainly sincere that no one was ever rude to him.

'Paul Merchant used to eat a lot of that stuff until he realised it was making him fat –and unfit,' commented Damian, pointing to the chocolate cake, as the others joined him at the table beside the leaded windows.

'No danger of that with me,' Ian replied confidently. 'I never put any weight on whatever I eat. I'm twice as fit as you – at least!'

Jonathan wasn't wasting eating-time on words: he was devouring his slice of treacle-and-currant tart with evident satisfaction. So far he'd hardly even glanced at Damian; it was almost as if he was embarrassed at being in his company. Damian, for his part, was wondering what had happened to Alex.

'Well, what are these ideas you've got about improving the team – in attack, anyway?' Damian inquired. He took only a small sip of his Coke because he was determined to make it last. He was desperately short of pocket money this week and he'd already had an advance on the following week's in order to buy some new football socks.

'I – well, we – think Jonathan here should move up front. He's got plenty of speed and he's the right height. I mean, that's just what we need most, isn't it?

Dalli-a-lot's got to have somebody to help him out and who else is there?'

Damian took a deep breath before replying. He'd watched a programme on mental and physical health and learned that it was very damaging to your system to explode with anger over anything. Take a deep breath and think carefully before speaking if you're upset: that was the advice he'd absorbed.

'I know this is saying the obvious,' he said in a deliberately slow tone, 'but Jonathan *is* our goalkeeper and, as far as I can remember, we don't have another goalkeeper. Am I right – '

'I wasn't *always* a goalie,' Jonathan put in quickly. 'I only took over last season because it was an emergency – you know, when your regular goalie was sent off. I used to be an outfield player and I was pretty good. Alex would back that up because we used to play in the same team when I scored quite a few goals. Well, I want to play up front again. I reckon I deserve the chance after all I've done for United.'

'But, Jonathan, we *need* you in goal. You've been brilliant there. You know – '

'You didn't say that last week!' Jonathan interrupted heatedly. 'You told me I *gave* Fyfield their last goal. You said I wasn't thinking about the game.'

'I don't think I put it quite like that, Jon,' Damian muttered, wishing now that he hadn't made that criticism.

'Well, maybe I *wasn't* thinking about goalkeeping,' Jonathan retaliated. 'I was probably thinking about getting really involved in the game in the middle of the park, not stuck out of the way between the posts. I think I've had goalkeeping up to here,' he added, putting the side of his hand against his throat.

'There is one other thing,' Ian said. 'Jonathan's a natural left-footer and you know we need somebody on the left flank. Well, with his height and speed *and* a good left foot he's exactly what we need. You know that's true, Damian. You've said the same thing yourself.'

Damian nodded. That couldn't be denied: United had to have a balanced team if they were to be successful. It had been in his mind to ask Alex Anson if he'd like to have a spell up front on the left flank because he was a two-footed player. But Alex was slightly built and didn't have much acceleration. He wouldn't be such a good prospect as Jonathan in that role.

'OK, I suppose we could give it a try,' the captain agreed reluctantly.'But what do we do about getting somebody else to play in goal? We haven't any spare players and nobody else has any experience between the sticks.'

There was a significant pause before Ian, after a quick glance at Jonathan, made his next suggestion.

'I think you should have a go in goal,' he said to Damian.

'What! I'm not even tall enough to be a goalie! And – and I'm needed in midfield. That's my best position.'

'You don't *have* to be tall to be a goalkeeper – you've

got to be alert and, and athletic. Ready to jump and throw yourself about,' Ian argued. 'Well, you're pretty fit, I'll admit that, and you can jump a good height. I've seen you.'

Damian was still flabbergasted by the idea. To give himself time to work out the implications he took a longer sip of his drink. Of one thing he was beginning to be sure: that Ian, aided by Jonathan, was scheming to take his place as captain of United. It wasn't easy to lead a team from the goalmouth and if that's where he found himself then it would be much easier for Ian to take charge in midfield and influence the rest of their team-mates.

'Look,' said Ian, impatient to know what Damian would decide to do, 'a good captain ought to be willing to play *anywhere*. Yes, anywhere, for the good of the team. I know I am – would be, I mean.'

'If it's an emergency then *of course* I'd be willing to play in goal,' Damian told them. 'But I think we ought to try to find an experienced goalkeeper if we can. We can sign up another player as long as he's not registered with any other team in the League.'

'There won't be time for that before next Sunday, even if you could find anybody good enough,' Ian countered.

'No, I don't suppose there is but we can start looking,' Damian agreed. He turned his attention to Jonathan. 'If you've been wanting to give up goalkeeping why didn't you say something before now? You could've mentioned it when we were together on

Sunday.'

Jonathan interlaced his fingers and then cracked his knuckles audibly. 'Well, everyone was a bit down after our match was cancelled. So I didn't want to make things worse. I was also, well, er, a bit keen to get away.'

'To play pool with Ian, I suppose,' said Damian. He watched the other two exchange glances but neither of them spoke. But it wasn't worth pursuing so he changed the subject. 'Do either of you know why Alex hasn't turned up?'

Ian shook his head. 'Not a clue. He didn't say anything to me about not coming to our committee meeting.'

'I've no idea, either, but I saw him at school today so he must be OK. Perhaps he's charged off to the beach to see if he can spot a Gigantic Red-necked Sand Dune Hopper,' joked Jonathan in a reference to Alex's hobby of ornithology.

'You weren't thinking of putting him in as goalie, were you?' Ian asked sharply.

'No, not – '

'He'd be absolutely *useless* there!' Jonathan razored in. 'He couldn't catch anything – not even a cold! I know, I've seen him try.'

'No, that wasn't what I was thinking at all,' Damian replied mildly. 'But I did want to ask his opinion about things, including whether we should try and find another coach. After all, Alex is vice-captain, you know.'

'No, I don't think we need anybody now – we can sort things out for ourselves,' Ian remarked. 'OK, I know we lost out last match, but Fyfield are a pretty fair side and now we've decided on some changes up front things'll improve. What do you think, Jon?'

'Oh sure, I agree. I mean, I'll be livening things up in the forward line and we could get a stack of goals against Brattleby.'

Damian wasn't at all sure about their coaching; Bryn had taught them a great deal and they were a much, much better side as a result. What's more, they had to make their own way in the League and the Cup. All the same, even European Champions had at least one coach on their staff, which proved that top professionals realised they still had things to learn.

'Well, I'm not too sure we oughtn't to have somebody to help out, even if it's only giving some advice occasionally,' he told them. 'It'd be useful just to have some grown-up around to support us and look after any player who's injured during a game. I believe that just having Bryn on the touch-line gave us confidence – even if he'd never said a word.'

'I suppose we could look around and see if anyone is available,' Ian said without much enthusiasm. 'It'd be different if any of the City players wanted the job, but they don't. So – '

'How do you know that?' Damian wanted to know.

'Bryn told me. He said he'd asked 'em but they're either fixed up with other teams or don't want to be bothered with junior football. We asked Bryn about it when we gave him the wallet.'

'Oh, I see,' was all Damian could say. He felt quite deflated.

'Well, look, I've got to go now,' said Ian, who had been eyeing some rich fruit cake; but he decided it might spoil his tea after all. 'But are you going to play in goal for us, Damian?'

'Well, yes, I suppose I'll have to. As you said, a captain's got to give a lead. But in this case I'll be leading from the back, won't I, not the front. And you can't get any further back than being in goal!'

'Great!' Ian declared, getting to his feet. 'But you'd better get some practice in before we play Brattleby. They may have a leaky defence but they've got some fairly big guys in their attack and they'll be trying to swarm all over you.'

'Yeah,' said Jonathan with a grin and holding out his hand to Damian. 'Best of luck.'

'Thanks a lot,' replied Damian rather dolefully as he accepted another handshake.

Five

As he pulled on the scarlet goalkeeper's jersey in the makeshift dressing-room at Coolington Sports Ground, Damian pondered on the problems he was going out to face. He'd been thinking about them for most of the week, ever since he'd agreed to go in goal, but thinking hadn't made them any easier. He was still fearful of making some utterly stupid error that would not only cost Darton United a goal but provoke gales of laughter at his expense. Like everyone else, apart from professional clowns, he didn't want to look idiotic.

During a couple of lunch-breaks at school he'd managed to persuaded Carl, a form-mate, to go with him to the remotest corner of the school grounds so that he could practise some saves. Carl, who played for a top team in another division of the Sunday League, was renowned for the power of his shooting; and Damian saw no point in trying to cope with anything but the best that could be fired at him. They had put coats down for the goal posts and Damian had flung himself around with enormous energy and determination. His luck was in because a couple of boys, who were passing by, wanted to join in and so the new goalkeeper was forced to deal with close-range headers and fling himself at players' feet in order to stifle tap-in shots almost on the line.

At the end of the first session he felt utterly exhausted and his shoulder ached from an accidental knock he'd taken from someone's shoe while he was trying to grab the ball. But Carl was very complimentary: 'Your handling's not bad and you showed a lot of guts. But things'll be different in a match, you know.'

Damian did know that. He realised that the real test would come when he was under pressure from a crowd of players during a corner kick or when a free kick was taken from the edge of the box. It wasn't so much his height, or lack of it, that was worrying him because he thought that his ability to jump well might compensate for that. One thing he couldn't train for was coming off his line at precisely the right moment to make an interception. A goalkeeper's sense of timing was instinctive: either that or it was developed and refined over a long period.

'Feeling nervous?' Ian asked with a crooked sort of grin as the players drifted out on to the pitch.

'Not much point in that, is there? If I feel nervous I'm bound to make mistakes. So I've got to feel confident. Then the rest of the defence will feel confident, too.'

Ian didn't make any reply but moved off with Jonathan to get some shooting-in practice that was clearly going to test Damian's reactions. Alex came to stand on the line beside his skipper. Damian had already asked him about his absence from the Canary Café meeting and Alex, giving nothing away, had merely said: 'Look, there's lots to tell you so let's have a talk after the match. We can go to my house if you like and you can eat with us.' That was such a surprise that Damian hadn't tried to question him any further.

When, a couple of minutes later, Damian went to the centre to toss-up, he saw that Ian hadn't been exaggerating when he described Brattleby's strikers as 'fairly big'. They looked like giants, towering over everyone else in their own side, so it was no wonder they'd scored a sackful of goals between them.

With the sun slanting across the pitch, Damian decided that he might as well let the other goalkeeper suffer its worst effects in the first half and so it was Brattleby who kicked off after losing the toss. There were several other matches taking place at the Coolington Ground, but Brattleby were unique in their choice of colours: chocolate-and-orange halved shirts and lighter brown shorts and socks. It was already, as one of the handful of spectators remarked in Damian's hearing, a colourful match. He hoped for an early touch of the ball to give him confidence in his handling: and he hadn't long to wait.

On their first real raid deep into United's half, Brattleby were awarded a free kick only a metre or so outside the box when Paul Merchant floored Matt Carter, the bigger of the two strikers. Damian had remonstrated with Paul after his feeble display in the

Fyfield match when the full-back was trying to avoid an injury before making his debut as a ball boy at the City Ground, and it seemed that Paul had learned his lesson. Now he was tackling with determination but, unhappily, without complete legality. Matt was accustomed to getting his own way against smaller opponents, but if ever they outwitted him or put in a clumsy tackle that caused him to lose the ball then he didn't hesitate to bellow that he'd been fouled. This time the referee had no option but to agree with him.

'Move over, move to the right!' Damian yelled to his defensive wall. He couldn't see anything of what was going on just outside the penalty area. If he didn't have some indication of where the shot was going his chances of saving it wouldn't be high. But, obstinately, the wall wouldn't co-operate; two opponents had joined in and the United defenders were rightly suspicious of their intentions.

At the last moment the Brattleby players duly broke away from the wall in a well-rehearsed movement and the ball, struck fiercely and accurately, came whistling through the gap they'd left. However, the kicker hadn't been able to keep it as low as he'd hoped and Damian was able to take the ball in his arms without having to move a centimetre. Even so, the force of the shot rocked him back on his heels and he was thankful he hadn't fumbled it as Matt Carter came bursting through the scattering defenders to challenge him.

'Well held, son,' said a voice behind the net as if he'd taken a catch on the boundary at cricket. Damian was genuinely pleased by the praise: it confirmed that he'd reacted well to his first test as a goalkeeper. Alex, too, nodded his approval and Damian nonchalantly bounced the ball a couple of times in his area before punting it well down the field. He'd been practising his drop-kicking and now he was able to achieve a good distance, though not as far as Jonathan could manage with his best efforts.

At the first opportunity, Ian Venn clipped the ball into Jonathan's path and yelled at him to run, run, run. So Jonathan ran, ran, ran – and no one seemed able to stop him as he swerved round one defender, cheekily nutmegged another and then cut into the penalty area. Damian, with his distant view of events, couldn't tell how close to the goalie Jonathan was before he fired in a shot; but, sadly for United, it was easily saved, the keeper plucking the ball out of the air as though reaching for an apple on a low branch. Nonetheless, Jonathan had every right to look pleased with his performance. Ian and one or two others applauded him heartily. It was obvious that he could control a ball, could run and was willing to take on defenders.

Most of all, it was the United forwards who were encouraged – and Neil Dallimore was inspired. Within moments of that McGuigan raid the ball was at Stevie Pailthorp's feet and he, too, decided to take on the Brattleby defence. Instead of passing to Ian, as Ian was demanding loudly and almost threateningly, Stevie sped down the touch-line, drew the full-back, put the ball past him on one side and scooted round him the other and then cut inside. The figure he'd picked out on the other flank to pass to was, naturally, Jonathan. The only trouble was that Stevie made his intention so clear to the Brattleby defenders that they had no trouble in intercepting that pass long before it might have reached Jonathan.

'I told you to give me the ball,' Ian complained bitterly. 'Do as you're told next time, Stevie.'

Stevie gave him a sharp look and made the predictable reply. 'You're not the captain. I don't have to obey your orders.'

'I'm thinking about *the team*,' Ian replied between clenched teeth. 'I was the nearest to you. Between us we could have ripped their defence wide open. And I had a better view than you.'

Those two raids had certainly given the chocolate-and-orange-shirted team the impression that United possessed some talented players; and, for the moment, their own attacking ambitions faded. Ian and Billy Sandford were beginning to dominate midfield and, whenever there was a fifty-fifty ball, it was one of them who emerged with it. To his astonishment, Damian was nothing more than a spectator; and he began to wish that he was playing up-front to capitalise on some of the mistakes their opponents were making.

Neutral observers – if such existed – wouldn't have been one whit surprised that, in the tenth minute of the match, Darton forced a succession of corners on the right. The first two were fruitless because the ball didn't even reach the goalmouth from Stevie's kicks but, for the third, the kick was taken by Ian who could unleash a lot of power when it was needed. Stevie hadn't argued when Ian asked, rather than demanded, to take the kick and he himself was the one who rose to head the ball when it came over at the perfect height. He was directing it towards the top right-hand corner of the net but, as the ball began to loop down, Jonathan, with faultless timing and initiative, jumped to divert it with his forehead into the opposite side of the net past the stranded goalkeeper.

The scorer was so ecstatic he actually turned a cartwheel – and then was mobbed by every Darton player who could reach him. It must, to the Brattleby team, have seemed like the winning goal in a Cup Final instead of simply being the first goal in a fairly ordinary Sunday League match.

'I told you this could happen!' Ian yelled to Damian when at last he returned to the centre circle for the re-start.

'Great!' Damian yelled back. He had advanced to the edge of his penalty area but knew it wasn't wise to go any further. Yet he wanted to caution his team to stay cool; one goal at this stage wasn't enough to guarantee victory. They needed another goal but, before that, they'd have to defend against Brattleby's inevitable determination to score the equalizer.

Billy, who was having an excellent game, stemmed the first onslaught with a timely tackle but only moments later the referee blew for an infringement when, unluckily, the ball struck Billy on the hand. Billy

naturally protested that it was an accident but the ref waved him away.

Unhappily, Billy couldn't accept that warning and, continuing to demand justice from the referee, was booked for dissent. 'Oh, you idiot!' Damian murmured under his breath. Now, if Billy committed another bookable offence, he'd be sent off and the team as a whole would suffer. In training sessions with Bryn their coach had emphasised umpteen times how stupid it was to try to argue with referees. 'It's the ref who *always* wins,' Bryn pointed out; but Billy seemed to have forgotten that.

A Brattleby full-back swung the ball into the goal-mouth. It was really a 'keeper's ball, to move out and jump for, but Damian had hesitated because he thought Paul Merchant was going to get there first and head it away. With the instinct of the striker for a half-chance Matt Carter flung himself headlong at the ball as it fell to waist height. What he couldn't control was his aim and all he succeeded in doing was turning the ball sideways towards Graeme Roustoby, his co-striker. Roustoby lunged at the ball just as Damian, deciding he must seize his chance, dived forward.

The Brattleby striker tumbled headlong over the goalkeeper as Damian tried to gather the ball which, in the mêlée, bounced out of his hands. Paul, recovering his composure after his own error of judgment, tried to clear the danger: but he missed the ball and instead his boot went into Damian's ribs. At the moment of impact Damian didn't realise how hard he'd been struck: his one concern was to grab the ball and, still on his knees, he reached out and succeeded in smothering it. Then, as he tried to get to his feet, he felt the fearful pain. Hugging the ball into his midriff, he sank to his knees again. The referee, spotting the contorted expression on Damian's face as he went down, promptly blew his whistle to stop the game.

'How do you feel, son?' he inquired with genuine concern as he tried to raise the injured player to his feet.

'Like death!' Damian gasped, which caused a couple of players to laugh and the ref to frown warningly. He knew from wide experience the kind of player who told the truth and the one who was a malingerer.

'Let's have a look at the damage,' said the ref, rolling up Damian's jersey and exploring his ribs with surprisingly tender fingers.

Damian, wincing with the pain of the blow and certain that something was smashed, found it hard even to stand upright. He didn't even realise he was still tightly clutching the ball until the ref, smilingly, persuaded him to surrender it to someone else.

'I don't *think* there's anything broken but if it stays very painful perhaps you ought to see your doctor,' the referee told him. 'Probably you'll just have a bad bruise there – a battle scar, if you like!'

Damian couldn't share in the smile but he was thankful the injury wasn't as bad as he'd feared. Perhaps, too, the pain was receding a little. At least he was able to stand up straight and walk about.

'D'you think you can carry on, son?' the referee

wanted to know. 'But don't try to be too brave just for the sake of it. If you feel in trouble we can certainly find somebody else to wear that smashing red jersey of yours.'

Damian could see that several of his players were looking alarmed at the possibility of being asked to take over in goal, though he noticed that Jonathan McGuigan was keeping well away from the penalty area. Doubtless he wanted to avoid the risk of having to resume his old role; and doubtless, too, he would claim that, now he was a goal-scorer, he was too valuable in the forward line to be replaced.

'You'll be all right, won't you, Damian?' Ian asked with a trace of anxiety in his voice.

Damian did momentarily think of saying that he'd be glad if Ian himself would take over but he sensed that Jonathan, for one, would simply believe that was a trick to put pressure on him (Jonathan) to volunteer. In any case, he suspected that Ian would be a hopeless goalkeeper because he lacked concentration – and he probably couldn't jump very high, either.

'I'll just about manage, I reckon,' Damian said to Ian's obvious relief. 'Oh, and who was it who whacked me?'

'Paul Merchant!' three players exclaimed simultaneously.

'Huh – the Merchant of Death,' joked Alex, remembering Damian's first words when the referee asked how he felt. Paul himself looked aghast but the rest of the group around Damian laughed.

'Well, next time, don't kick me, kick one of the opposition,' Damian told the moon-faced full-back.

By now the game was about to be re-started with what the referee had decided should be a free kick, although that was hardly a strict interpretation of the rules as no Brattleby player had committed any offence; but he wasn't going to drop the ball on the goal-line and risk another injury to the goalkeeper.

Fortunately for Damian, who was trying to ease the pain by massaging his rib cage, the ball was detained in midfield for two or three minutes as both sides struggled to dominate the game. Brattleby had the feeling that the fates were against them and none of their players had the confidence to retain possession and outwit opponents with sheer ball skills.

Then the deadlock was broken by the unexpected enterprise of Stevie Pailthorp who, up to that moment, had contributed hardly anything to the game, not least because Ian was tending to feed Jonathan on the left flank rather than Stevie on the right. It was this sense of isolation that made the speedy winger keep possession when he picked up a sliced clearance; he had plenty of energy in reserve and he was going to use some of it up. The mazy run he began was a revelation to his team-mates as well as to Brattleby. He edged in to the penalty area and then out again; seemed to make for the corner flag but then back-tracked to the eighteen-yard line; and then, after defeating two attempted tackles with quite audacious sleight-of-foot, he suddenly accelerated into top gear, swerved round the last defender and, noting the goalkeeper's uncertainty, fired a fierce shot that kept low and stayed on target all the way. A second before the goalie decided to dive, the ball was zipping past him on its way into the far bottom corner of the net.

Even Stevie himself seemed to find it hard to believe that he'd scored such a goal. Open-mouthed at his own accomplishment he stood, transfixed, as, first, spectators erupted into loud applause and, second, his team-mates rushed towards him to submerge him in praise.

'Fantastic goal!' Ian exclaimed. 'Out of this world!'

That seemed the right description. The Brattleby players were actually walking around, blinking or shaking their heads, as if they'd just arrived from another planet. Even the referee, after making a note in his book, made a point of going up to Stevie to say: 'Well done, son. That was a fine achievement. Pity the television cameras weren't here to record it!'

When, three minutes later, the whistle shrilled for half-time, Steve Pailthorp's goal was still all anybody could talk about. Because he was modest by nature he didn't care for all the fuss and he insisted: 'Look I didn't *know* I was going to score like that when I picked the ball up. I mean, it just, well, sort of *happened*. I could've missed just as easily, couldn't I?'

'Well, that's sewn the game up, no danger,' Ian chortled. 'We ought to get plenty more goals in the second half because they're shell-shocked. Don't know what's hit 'em!'

'I think they'll be pretty dangerous in the second half,' Damian declared. 'They'll have to attack, won't they, because they've got nothing to lose now they're two down.'

'Aw, come on, *skipper*, you can do better than that!' Ian said with plain sarcasm. 'Don't start talking as though we're going to *lose*. When we're winning like we are you should look on the bright side.'

Damian, who was munching his potassium-rich banana to ward off any risk of fatigue, shook his head violently. He was beginning to get tired of Ian's assumption that he was the only one with all the answers.

'You didn't listen to what I said,' he told him. 'I'm just being realistic. But at soccer, anything can happen. You should know that.'

'Complacent, that's what teams can get when they're in front,' Alex Anson put in much to Damian's surprise. 'We musn't be complacent. If we do we're in trouble. I agree with what Damian said.'

Damian gave him a grateful look and waited to see what Ian would come up with next. But the midfielder simply shrugged his shoulders and then went into a huddled chat with Jonathan for the remainder of the interval.

In fact, Damian's prediction was totally accurate. Brattleby began the second half as if they'd been threatened with execution if they didn't score a quick goal. Graeme Roustoby appeared determined to emulate Stevie's feat and he almost succeeded. His run, however, was more direct but he shrugged off the attentions of Ian and Billy and then sent Paul the wrong way with a delightful dummy before hammering in a ferocious shot. Afterwards Damian wondered how he'd reached the ball but somehow he managed to palm it against the angle of the upright and the crossbar: and when it rebounded he gratefully caught it.

'You lucky devil!' Roustoby yelled at him and Damian could hardly deny it. For once luck did seem to be on his side.

That was only the first in a wave of attacks and Damian guessed that his luck couldn't hold out for ever, especially after he'd diverted one shot to safety with his heel while lying on the ground after a mêlée. The United defence had been doing their best to protect him in every way and Alex had never played better or more intelligently; he seemed to know what an opponent was going to do before the opponent himself knew. In contrast, Matt Carter was having absolutely no luck at all and then, when presented with an open goal, he mis-kicked completely and skyed the ball over the bar. Damian was just starting to feel that being a stand-in goalkeeper wasn't so terrible after all when Brattleby got their long-awaited goal and he took another painful knock. This time the referee could do nothing to help him: and, in any case, in his opinion the goalkeeper had acquitted himself exceptionally well in his new role.

For once the full-backs were caught unawares as Roustoby pounced on a poor pass from a team-mate and sprinted clear of everyone into the penalty area. Damian, on his line, now experienced the goalie's classic dilemma.

His instinct was to stay on his line and hope that the striker would hit his shot within reach; but then he decided he must rush out to unsettle him and try to grab the ball. He very nearly succeeded in his aim but Graeme was cool enough to pull the ball back as Damian dived and then take it round the prone goalkeeper before sliding it into the net. Yet, as he did so, Damian's despairing hand caught his ankle and Graeme, knocked off balance, fell backwards on top of his opponent. For the second time in the match Damian had the breath squashed out of him and pain came flooding back. Graeme, of course, was on his feet in an instant and charging back to the centre, waving his arms in glee at putting Brattleby back into the game.

'You nearly got there and stopped the goal,' Alex told his captain. 'Honestly, you were a bit unlucky.'

Damian, receiving further ministrations from the concerned referee, shook his head. 'I don't agree,' he said when at last he could speak again. 'My timing was wrong. Goalkeeping isn't my game, I've decided.'

But, after Darton had hung on, if at times precariously, for a 2–1 victory, the rest of the team tried to convince the skipper that he'd not only done a fine job in goal but brought them some welcome luck. The overwhelming view was that he should stay between the posts for the remainder of the season.

'No way!' Damian replied decisively. 'I think *I* was lucky, apart from getting bashed about. We need a goalkeeper who *really* knows what he's doing all the time and isn't just hoping for the best. So if Jonathan is going to stay up front we'll have to find somebody else.'

Six

Damian took a long sniff. 'Hey, that smells good, *really* good!' he exclaimed. 'What is it?'

'Nut roast, I expect,' answered Alex, slinging his sports bag neatly on to a couple of coat hooks in the hall. 'It's what we usually have on a Sunday.'

'Nuts! What sort of nuts?' was the disbelieving question.

'Oh, I don't know: hazel, brazil, walnuts, all sorts. You can mix 'em up and get lots of different flavours. If we're lucky we might get some chips as well. I know they're not supposed to be good for you but Mum often makes some just for me.'

Mrs Anson appeared in the kitchen doorway at that moment to greet them, brushing strands of her long, black hair away from her eyes with the back of the hand that was holding a wooden spoon.

'Hi, nice to see you, Damian. I'm glad you're here because I've kept telling Alex it was time he brought his boss home for lunch!'

'Boss?' Damian was genuinely baffled.

'Well, you're the captain, aren't you? And Alex is vice-captain, right? So you're in charge. Alex is a great one for chains of command in my experience. He thinks highly of you, Damian.'

'Oh,' was all Damian could say. He glanced at his friend but Alex didn't look to be embarrassed in the slightest. He went up to his mother to give her a kiss and then ask if Damian could phone home to say that he was lunching out. Of course, he was told, and Mrs Anson pointed to the study before returning to the kitchen to put the chips on.

Mrs Tennant seemed relieved to hear her son's news because, she said, she was leaving early for an important badminton tournament and Damian's father was away playing golf all day.

'So they didn't want me around anyway,' Damian said to Alex with wry amusement. 'Listen, I didn't know you thought much about being vice-captain. I got the idea you felt it was meaningless.'

'Oh no!' Alex, reclining in his father's black leather office chair, replied indignantly. 'It's my job to back you up at all times.'

'Well, I didn't notice you backing me up at the Canary Café meeting. You didn't even turn up!'

'That was on purpose,' Alex explained solemnly. 'You see, Ian hoped I would help him and Jonathan get rid of you as captain. No, hang on! Let me finish. It's been obvious to everybody that Ian wants to be captain again. He got Jonathan on his side and he thought that would influence me to support him as well because Jon

and I used to be mates. But Jonathan's got big-headed and is going around with a different crowd now. So – '

'But if you'd turned up at the meeting you could just have stood by me and said what you've said now,' Damian cut in.

Alex shook his head. 'No, that wouldn't have worked. Ian wanted to have a vote. If you and I had voted together against those two it would have been 2–2. But that would have caused a bad split and more trouble in the future. It was best to make sure there wasn't going to be a vote at all. Don't you see that, Damian?'

'Well yes, now you've explained it. But I expect it'll happen again in the future so it might have been best to have sorted it out then at the Canary.'

Again Alex disagreed. 'I don't think it will crop up again. The rest of the team really admire you for taking over in goal. They think that shows real leadership. I know because I've been round everybody, asking them what they think. If there was a vote you'd win at least 9–2. They wouldn't want Ian as captain because they know he wouldn't have become the goalie.'

'He said he would!'

'Maybe he did. But he didn't mean it. Ian's always willing to say anything to get what he wants. I'll tell you something else, Damian: Ian claimed he'd got you to go between the sticks because you couldn't shout at him from there! He hated it when you told him off but you were right to do it. You see, Ian only thinks of himself but you, well, you think of the *team*. That's why you're a good leader and Ian never would be.'

Before Damian could reply Mrs Anson called them to lunch and he was introduced to Alex's younger brother, Scott, who looked even more studious than Alex usually did. The nut roast and *mange tout* and chips were as delicious as anything Damian had ever eaten and, because he was ravenous after the game, he was thankful there was enough of everything for second helpings.

'Look, if you two want to natter away about soccer, that's fine by us,' Mrs Anson remarked. 'Alex normally doesn't get much chance of that because the rest of us aren't exactly mad keen supporters. Alex apart, we aren't a sporty family, except for the odd game of ping-pong.'

'Table tennis, Mum!' Alex corrected her fiercely, but his mother merely laughed.

'Look, do you reckon Jonathan is determined not to play in goal any more?' asked Damian, taking up Mrs Anson's invitation.

'Oh sure. Now he's scored a goal he'll want to become a striker. He always did fancy himself as a great goal-scorer.'

'Well, in that case, we'll just have to find another goalie. But where do we begin . . .?'

He paused as Mrs Anson gave him a generous portion of lemon meringue pie which proved to be too good to linger over.

'I think I can help,' Alex disclosed. 'There's a lad from our school who plays in Saturday games for Farnfield. They play at Sundial Hill near you and I think Hajinder is pretty good. If you went to watch him next Saturday you could see what you think and then talk to him.'

'Great! We could go together and – '

'No, sorry, I can't,' Alex interrupted. 'You see Scott is playing his fiddle in a concert in Peterborough and the whole family's promised to go and support him. As I say, I've seen Hajinder but it's what you think that matters. You're the skipper. Anyway, now you've played in goal yourself you'll know exactly what to look for.'

'You can say that again!' Damian responded feelingly, tenderly exploring his ribs.

Seven

Standing under the shower in the bathroom at home, Damian was alternating the hot water with the cold and gasping with exaggerated pleasure at each temperature change. The hot-and-then-cold water treatment was, he'd read, excellent for toning up the whole body and especially beneficial to sportsmen. Although he wasn't playing in any game that day he'd decided he might as well test the idea and see how he felt as a result.

He was just about to switch off when his mother walked in.

'Hey,' he exclaimed, 'I thought bathrooms were supposed to be private places!'

'Oh, that's just an old-fashioned idea,' she replied airily. 'Anyway, you can't have any secrets from me. I've known you since you were born! Oh, and you were making such a row I feared you were drowning or something.'

Damian grinned and, stepping out of the stall, took the towel his mother had removed from the heated rail. 'I was just proving how terrifically fit I am,' he said, starting to rub his hair dry.

'Damian! What on earth have you been up to? How did you get that colossal bruise on your side – and that other one on your leg? You haven't been fighting have you?'

He was taken aback by her concern; so far as he was concerned the yellow and purple patches were fading nicely and the pain had just about gone. But then he realised she hadn't seen them before.

'Oh, I just took a couple of minor knocks when I was goalkeeper last week,' he said dismissively. 'Honestly, they're fine now, Mum. It was just a bit of bad luck at the time.'

'Honestly, I'd no idea football was such a dangerous game. If that's what – '

'Mum, I told you: it was just bad luck and I wasn't used to being in goal. And I won't be again if everything goes well today. That's why you're dropping me off at Sundial Hill, so that I can find a replacement goalkeeper.'

His mother gave him a doubting glance. 'Well, it had better go well. I don't want to see you covered in bruises again, darling. Sport should be for pleasure, not physical endurance and pain. Now listen, I want to be away from here in five minutes. So you'd better get some clothes on pretty smartly.'

Of course, she was in a hurry because she was going to play yet another badminton game, but Damian didn't mind leaving earlier than he'd planned because it would give him time to see more football at Sundial

Hill, where, on a Saturday, as many as a dozen matches would be taking place.

'You're very quiet,' his mother remarked in the car. 'You're not worrying about anything, are you? I mean, if it's your football with all these problems about injuries and other people wanting to be captain, maybe you *ought* to give it up. The captaincy, I mean. Then you'd probably start enjoying the game again.'

'No way!' Damian replied emphatically. 'I'm going to go on being captain and everybody knows that – or they soon will. I'm going to lift United, even if I have to do *everything* myself.'

'But your friend Alex is going to help, isn't he? I think it was very thoughtful the way he took you off to lunch at his home last Sunday.'

'Oh, sure, Alex is going to help. But it's up to me to make all the important decisions. Well, this'll do fine, Mum – and thanks a lot for the lift. Hope you win *your* game.'

He thought about Alex as he wandered between the games, looking for the one in which Hajinder was taking part. Until the previous weekend he'd never appreciated how much United meant to Alex and the degree of loyalty that he possessed. But for Alex's clever move in absenting himself from the Canary Café meeting, a deep division might have appeared within the ranks of the United players with Ian and Jonathan trying to win votes for Ian as captain. Instead, he had played creditably in goal (Damian saw no point in being falsely modest), Jonathan had demonstrated that he *could* play up front and team spirit was excellent. Now, if they kept on winning, no talk about changing captains could possibly be justified.

As it turned out, he timed his arrival beautifully. His first view of Hajinder was as the scarlet-sweatered goalkeeper flung himself bodily across the goalmouth to turn a shot round the post. Then, from the resulting corner, he jumped bravely through a crowd of attackers to punch the ball effectively out of the area. Because he himself had twice failed to connect when trying to punch the ball clear the previous Sunday Damian was impressed by Hajinder's effort. A few moments later the ball was at the other end of the pitch and so, when Hajinder glanced round, Damian gave him an encouraging smile and called: 'Terrific save you made there.'

Hajinder nodded his thanks but didn't allow his concentration to lapse in spite of the fact that play was going entirely in favour of his team. Damian had already spotted some skilful ball control by one of their forwards who seemed to have plenty of time to do whatever he wanted to do, whether it was to pass or take on an opponent or to shoot. That, he knew, was always the mark of a talented player. Damian started to wonder whether he, too, was free to join United.

Damian waited until half-time before he made any approach to Hajinder and even then he inquired whether the goalkeeper was needed to take part in any team talk. But, it turned out, he wasn't; and, it also turned out, he wasn't too keen on playing for United when Damian, after introducing himself and mentioning his friendship with Alex, broached the subject.

'You're not doing very well, are you?' he pointed out. 'I look at the League tables regularly so I know where you are. Only just in the top half. Yes?'

Damian had anticipated that answer. 'That's because we need a top-class goalie like you, Hajinder. We've been letting in too many goals. You'd've stopped nearly all the ones that Jonathan let in. Oh, and the one that got past me last Sunday, too.'

Hajinder didn't respond immediately to such flattery. He appeared to be pondering some point. Damian decided he must press his case as enthusiastically as possible. If Hajinder turned them down Damian hadn't a clue who else he might approach.

'All the rest of the team are dead keen to have you in the side,' he added. 'You'd give us all bags of confidence.'

Hajinder began pulling at the lobe of his left ear, something his father always did when he was being persuasive. 'If I agreed, then you'd have to keep me in goal for every match. Whatever happens.'

Damian stared. 'What, even if you, er, had a run of bad games – made a lot of mistakes?'

'That's right. You're not allowed to drop me, not for any reason.'

'But not even the captain of England is guaranteed his place in the team for *every* match,' Damian pointed out. 'Managers are always telling top players that they still have to play for their places. The manager of Arsenal said last week that a player's only as good as his last match. I know, I heard him on the radio myself.'

'But you're not a manager,' Hajinder said softly.

'I know, but I'm the captain. I pick the team, more or less.'

'Then,' Hajinder said triumphantly, 'there's no problem, is there? You just keep choosing me and no one can argue.'

'Well, I don't know about that, Haji. There's a bit of a risk in it and – '

'But you just said yourself that I'm a top class goalie. So how can you speak of risks?'

Damian paused, reflecting. 'Well, I mean, you could suffer a loss of form. That could happen to anybody. Even the captain of England. Look, I'll have to think about this, Haji.'

The dark-skinned boy shrugged. 'Well, please yourself, my friend.' He hesitated and then added: 'Anyway, Scale Hill Colts, are *really* interested in me.'

'Have they actually asked you to play for them?' Damian wanted to know.

'Almost. They said they'd be round to sign me up as soon as their regular goalkeeper left. His family's moving to London, you see.'

Damian scratched his head, trying to remember something. 'Isn't that Tony Hooberry?' he asked.

'Perhaps,' said Haji indifferently.

'Well, he won't be leaving for a long time!' Damian

announced with some satisfaction. 'His Dad's decided not to move after all. Mrs Hooberry says she can't bear the thought of leaving Darton. I know that because she meets my Mum at the Leisure Centre. They play badminton together. Sometimes she comes to our house.'

'Oh' said Hajinder, defeated for the moment.

But at that point negotiations had to be suspended anyway because the referee was signalling the start of the second half.

Hajinder was soon in action and dealt very competently with a couple of long-range shots as well as an almost suicidal back pass from one of his side's central defenders. Certainly he wasn't afraid to throw himself about when necessary and the risk of getting kicked in a mêlée didn't deter him. There were moments when he appeared to have a nonchalant, almost arrogant, attitude towards his role; but Damian knew that a confident player was a skilful player. In any case, he had an idea that Hajinder was simply showing off in order to try and impress him.

Eventually, however, Damian decided he ought to see what else was going on. After all, if he was here as a scout then he should be sizing up other possible signings for United. Hajinder's remark that Damian wasn't a manager had had the effect of making him realise that he was virtually in complete charge of the team. Nobody argued about his selections: or, at least, not until recently when Ian suggested changes and Jonathan elected to play as a striker. So if he could now provide them with a reliable goalkeeper and perhaps one other new player his position as captain would be beyond any challenge.

Of all the players he saw while strolling round the various pitches at Sundial none could really begin to compare with the striker he'd noticed in Hajinder's team. Long-legged rather than just tall, he made whatever he did look remarkably simple. There was economy of effort and precision in all his moves and when he scored his side's winning goal a couple of minutes from the end of the game with a deft lob over the goalkeeper's outstretched arms Damian instinctively applauded. Yet the scorer himself seemed quite unconcerned about his achievement.

He was behind Hajinder's goal again when the match came to an end and by then Damian had decided that United had found the goalkeeper they needed. His one problem now was to convince Hajinder that he would be doing the best for himself by joining Darton.

But, to his surprise, Hajinder had already reached his own decision.

'I've noticed you studying other goalkeepers today,' he said, coming to stand close to Damian and look him straight in the eyes. 'Am I the best you've seen?'

'Yes, definitely,' Damian replied truthfully.

'In that case, I will play for your Darton United. I think you are an honest person and you will play fair with me. So I will always play my best for the team.'

'Great!' Damian was delighted. Then, quickly, he added: 'Look, I'll fill you in on all the details about

Darton after you've got changed. But what's the name of the boy who scored the winning goal for you?'

'Warren Snowball.'

'What! I don't – '

'It's true! But you mustn't make jokes about his name. He hates that, though some of the boys call him Icy and he doesn't mind that, I think. We all think he is a very cool player, you see.'

'Yeah, you can say that again,' Damian agreed. 'D'you know if he plays for anybody in the Sunday League?'

Hajinder shook his head. 'I doubt that. He has, you see, only just come to live in this town. So I think he will not have made many friends yet. Also, he is a bit of a loner, doesn't mix with many people.'

'Well, could you tell him I'd like a word? I'll wait for you both to get changed.'

'OK, Damian, we won't be long,' Hajinder promised before dashing off to the distant changing-rooms.

When they met, a few minutes later, Damian wasn't at all surprised by the nickname Warren had been given. His eyes were a startling light grey and his look distinctly cool and rather calculating. Yet his voice and his manner were friendly enough when he responded to Damian's invitation to join Darton United.

'Sure, I'm interested. I wanted to play regularly when I came to Redbourne. But I was off sick for three weeks and I didn't get the chance. Are United any good? I mean, I don't want to go to a useless team. I want to be with a team that's going to win things.'

'Oh, yes, I'm the same!' Damian told him emphatically. 'Darton are definitely getting better all the time. We had a bad time last season but then we got Bryn Marsden as coach and he made a terrific difference to us. He also arranged for the rest of the team to be ball boys at the Plymouth match and I was mascot. So we're really ambitious, Warren. With you and Hajinder in the side I reckon we can be the best in the Division.'

Warren nodded, his eyes now beginning to glow a little with enthusiasm. 'Can you – we – get promotion this season?'

'I don't see why not, if we keep winning. There are enough matches left to get the points we need. Tell you what: come to the Canary Café after school next Tuesday. Both of you, I mean. Then you can meet Alex Anson – well, I think you already know him, Haji. He's our vice-captain. And there'll be a couple of other players there, too, Ian Venn, who plays in midfield alongside me and Jonathan McGuigan, who is also, er, a striker. We can really get down to talking about tactics and future matches and things like that.'

'Sounds a good idea,' Warren commented. 'Let's do that, then. Do you think there's a chance I might get invited to be City's mascot?'

'Er, I've no idea,' Damian confessed. 'Now that Bryn's gone we don't have the same contact with City. But, well, I suppose it's possible if we can keep in touch with the club.'

Warren had noticed, though Damian hadn't, that a

car was making its way along the boundary of the sports area towards them. It pulled up alongside them and the front passenger door was opened.

'This is my dad, come to pick me up,' Warren said off-handedly. 'And Hajinder, too. See you then, Damian.'

Damian waved them off. It didn't occur to him that he hadn't been offered a lift home; but then he didn't really want one. He was going to enjoy a walk further up Sundial Hill, just on his own. After all, he had a lot to think about: a lot of good things. With his friend Alex's help he had, that morning, become a successful football scout. From now on, with Hajinder and Warren in their ranks, Darton United would be a very successful Sunday League team. Of that, Damian had no doubt at all.

Eight

Everyone was listening to Damian, and listening with some attention. Damian himself was feeling nervous, more nervous than he'd ever been in his life he thought, and that was why he was pacing up and down the changing-room as he talked about the game ahead of them. They were playing Ellel Thistle, the Division leaders, and Damian was describing it as the most important match in Darton United's history.

'If we win this one it'll show everybody that we have to be taken seriously as promotion candidates,' he insisted, punching one fist into the palm of his hand in an unconscious imitation of one of Bryn Marsden's mannerisms. 'It'll show that we have *really* arrived.'

'It'll also show Thistle that they aren't as sharp as they think they are!' joked Neil Dallimore, and nearly everyone laughed. And that helped to reduce the tension.

Neil had every reason to feel in good humour because he was one of the players who had benefited most from the arrival of Warren Snowball, the boy with the

unbelievable name and the talent that sometimes had to be seen to be believed. His unselfish play had set up several goal-scoring chances for Neil which even he, in his most erratic form, could hardly miss. Of course, he still had managed to miss a few but he'd put the rest away with deep satisfaction. Warren was inclined to play just behind Neil and Jonathan, the two front-runners, and the opposition hadn't always worked out quickly enough just how dangerous he was as the real creator of chances.

'Well, I'm glad we're all in a good mood,' Damian concluded, 'because if we aren't at our best we won't beat this lot. But if we can get an early goal and really rattle 'em then we'll win. Then we can really start thinking about promotion. So, good luck boys.'

As they ran out on to the pitch Damian had a last word with Warren. 'It'd be nice if you could get a goal yourself today, Warren. Be a good way of breaking your duck with United.'

'Yeah, I suppose so,' Warren replied but without much enthusiasm for the idea. 'But it doesn't matter who scores our goals as long as we win, does it?'

Damian had to agree with that view because it was part of his own football philosophy; nonetheless, he wished that sometimes Warren would add a sharper edge to his skills by displaying a real desire to put the ball in the net himself. For some reason he didn't possess what Damian had heard a famous professional describe as 'the killer touch – the determination to finish off things that you've started'. Warren could hardly be called lazy because he was always willing to work as hard as was necessary to set up incisive attacks; but once the opening had been made he was inclined to let others take over. Since he'd joined them three weeks earlier United hadn't been beaten, though they'd won only one match. It had crossed Damian's mind to ask Warren to play as an out-and-out striker and see what happened then. But so far he'd resisted the temptation, not least because he didn't want to risk upsetting the regular strikers. Warren himself might have turned the idea down flat on the grounds that he regarded himself as a play-maker, not a centre-forward.

Thistle, too, possessed a player of star quality in

midfield: a dark-haired, rather plump boy called Ben Shaw who, in addition to carving out openings for their strikers, managed to feature quite regularly on the score sheet. At a team meeting earlier that week Ian had actually volunteered to mark Ben throughout the match. 'I'll cover him like a blanket!' he'd promised. Damian, approving of that determination, had also wondered whether Stevie Pailthorp might provide support, too, but he hadn't liked to suggest it in case Ian felt his marking abilities were being questioned. Yet it was common knowledge in the League that much of Ellel's success could be traced back to Ben's skills and perception of the game.

As usual Thistle, in their dark blue shirts, white shorts and red socks, had attracted a good crowd to their home match and it was rumoured that among the spectators were League officials and at least one talent scout. They didn't have to wait long for something to cheer, for the first goal was scored within sixty seconds of the kick-off. It was, of course, Ben Shaw who set up the chance with a finely-judged pass to the right flank, where the winger eluded a rather careless tackle and then sent in a good cross. There should have been no danger for United because Alex Anson was under no pressure at all and should have been able to head the ball away with ease. Instead, the normally dependable Alex headed it straight to the feet of an in-rushing forward who was alert enough to check his momentum and then hit the ball cleanly and unstoppably past Hajinder's right hand. The goalkeeper hadn't had a chance of making a save as he told everyone within earshot; but he hardly needed to because no one was blaming him.

Alex, naturally, was mortified. 'I can't believe it happened,' he muttered. 'It's a total disaster!'

'No, it isn't!' Damian told him fiercely. 'It could happen to anybody. You've saved dozens of goals in other matches. So just forget it. Alex. *Forget it!*'

Thistle, understandably, now had the idea that they were going to enjoy a goal-rush and their supporters began to applaud every kick and every move. For the next few minutes Ben Shaw was really fizzing, popping up everywhere to take a pass or give one and then, with the goal in his sights, to fire in a bullet of a shot that Hajinder, who only saw it at the last moment, somehow managed to palm over the bar.

Ian, who thought he'd managed to shackle Ben moments earlier, but was defeated by a brilliant 360-degree turn, pulled a face in frustration when Damian gave him a questioning look. The skipper signalled to Stevie Pailthorp to help out as Thistle took what proved to be an unproductive corner.

'You're our fastest runner,' Damian said hurriedly. 'If Shaw gets away from Ian at any point then go after him – pin him down.'

Stevie nodded his understanding. For the next few minutes United's goal was simply under siege as Thistle, determined to get the second goal they believed would clinch the match for them, swarmed all over the penalty area. Warren had dropped back and was doing his best to mark another of Ellel's danger men when the ball, ricocheting from an opponent's knee, struck his hand. Instantaneously, the referee's whistle shrilled.

'Oh no, ref!' Warren protested vigorously, for once losing his icy demeanour. 'It was a pure accident!'

But the referee wouldn't agree and was pointing calmly at the penalty spot as Thistle players told each other jubilantly that it was only what they deserved.

To Damian's surprise, the controversy seemed not to be bothering Hajinder. Rubbing his gloved hands together, he stationed himself on his line, looking quite nerveless. Although he hadn't been aware of it before, Damian sensed now that a crisis simply brought the best out of their new goalkeeper. 'Best of luck, Haji,' he called out as the kicker placed the ball on the spot; but it was doubtful if Hajinder heard him. His concentration on what was happening directly in front of him was total.

The penalty was being taken by Ellel's captain, a centre back with a powerful kick, and he'd selected a spot just inside the right-hand post. By some feat of mind-reading Hajinder guessed exactly where the ball was going and flung himself in that direction as the ball was kicked. He actually managed to get both hands to the ball and though he couldn't hold it he diverted it against the upright. As it spun upwards Haji, scrambling to his feet, dived again to grasp it – and then crashed shoulder-first into the woodwork.

By the time Haji collapsed, prone, on the goal-line

practically all the other players had rushed into the penalty area, those in blue shirts with the faint hope of being able to prod the ball over the line. But it was still firmly in Haji's arms in spite of the pain from his injured shoulder. The referee and Warren's father, who brought several of the boys to the match in his car, were the first to go to the goalkeeper's assistance and discover how bad the injury was.

'Well, I'm sure there's nothing broken, son, but I think we'd better take you off to the hospital for them to have a look at it,' said Mr Snowball, who admired the goalkeeper's determination not to give up the ball until he had to; there were tears in Haji's eyes but he was really being very brave.

'That really was a terrific save – the best I've ever seen,' Damian told him as Hajinder was helped out of his scarlet jersey. 'You've kept us in the game.'

'I'll be back, Damian,' Hajinder promised as he was led away to Mr Snowball's car, a jacket wrapped round his thin shoulders.

'Oh, good grief!' Damian exclaimed, using an expression his mother favoured when she lost a vital point at badminton or a crisis occurred in her household. He had suddenly realised what Hajinder's departure meant. 'I suppose *I'll* have to take over in goal now.'

'No, it's *my* job,' Jonathan put in unexpectedly, holding out his hand for the red jersey. 'I'm the stand-in goalkeeper, remember? We need you in midfield, Damian.'

Damian did his best to conceal his astonishment. 'Oh, thanks, Jon. I'm glad you're taking over.'

These days United could enjoy the luxury of a substitute and Damian now waved to Billy Sandford, who had the role for this match, to come on to the field and give his name to the referee. He was going to give Billy his old place back in midfield and ask Warren to move up to partner Neil Dallimore as a striker.

'OK, I'll try it, but don't expect a net-full of goals from me,' Warren replied.

'Just two will do,' Damian grinned.

But it was some minutes before United even got into the other half of the field. Ellel seemed desperate to make up for the goal they'd missed when Hajinder saved the penalty and their strikers, prompted by the still effervescent Ben Shaw, bombarded Jonathan with shots from all distances. Jonathan, though, was giving the impression that he'd spent his entire life between the posts. His agility and his handling were faultless.

Yet, in spite of their dominance, Thistle couldn't get the second goal they knew they needed. As half-time approached it was obvious that Ben Shaw was becoming less effective at setting up attacks; at last, Ian Venn was getting the upper hand in their personal battle. Ben, tired of being marked out of the game by someone he regarded as an inferior player, rashly kicked out and caught Ian on the knee. Ian, inevitably, made the most of it with a pantomime of pain and passion as he writhed on the ground. Of course he wasn't seriously hurt but he won a free kick, a sympathetic pat from the referee and, in effect, a booking for the offender.

It was from that kick just inside the United half that the visitors produced their best attacking move so far. Damian sent the ball curling towards the edge of the box where Neil out-jumped all the opposition to nod the ball down to Warren who immediately flicked it on to Billy Sandford. Delighted to be in the action at last, Billy had the good sense to return the compliment and Warren, cutting inside the challenging full-back, drove the ball towards the top of the net with his left foot. Unfortunately for United, Thistle's goalkeeper proved to be every bit as competent as Hajinder and Jonathan. Although he'd started to advance as danger threatened he recovered fast enough to fist the ball just as it was passing over his head and send it to safety high over the bar.

Ian, who'd swiftly got over his knock on the knee, took the corner kick and played it short to Stevie. Jinking one way and then the other, the winger beat two defenders and then hammered the ball into the middle. Neil wasn't so much the target as in the way because the ball was intended for Warren. Instead of jumping over the ball, which would have completely fooled the opposition, Neil swung heartily at it – and fairly predictably sent it on an apparent mission to the moon.

Damian raised his eyes skywards, too, but didn't utter a word of criticism. He knew that Neil didn't respond to hard words but only to praise.

During the interval the United players drank tea

from vacuum jugs and ate sugary biscuits kindly provided by Ellel supporters; and talked non-stop about their prospects of getting some League points from this match. Ian even apologised to his skipper for getting booked but promised that he'd be just as determined in the second half to subdue Ben Shaw. Warren Snowball was really the only one who had nothing to say and Damian suspected he might be brooding – either about giving away the penalty or being asked to play as a striker. So he asked what was troubling him.

'Just trying to work out how we're going to win, that's all,' was the grey-eyed boy's response. 'You know, I think there's not much between us. I think the main difference is that they expect to win every game and we don't. Maybe that's why they are top of the division.'

That wasn't at all the insight Damian had expected. 'I reckon you could be right,' he agreed. 'So we'll just have to prove we can be winners, too. Are you happy about playing up-front?'

Warren nodded. 'Sure. It's a new challenge. And I like challenges.'

Thistle, however, were the first to attack in the second half. In spite of the close attentions of Ian, Ben Shaw managed to send a superlative pass to his right-winger and he, in turn, supplied the centre-forward with exactly the kind of ball he liked: one that he could pounce on as he accelerated. His pace took him past two defenders with ease. Jonathan, sensing what could happen, didn't hesitate for even a second.

He charged from his goal, arms spread wide, determined to smother any attempted shot or as least put the striker under pressure so that he made a fatal mistake. Thistle's centre-forward, however, was cool enough to drag the ball to one side, out of the goalie's reach he hoped, before trying to hook it into the net with his left foot. He might have succeeded if Jonathan hadn't caught his ankle with the very tips of his fingers, a contact that sent him rolling over and over. It was the goalie who was first on his feet to grab the loose ball, but by then the referee's whistle had shrilled. And the official was again pointing to the penalty spot.

'Oh no, not *again*!' Damian groaned. 'It was just an accident, like the last time.'

Predictably, the referee would listen to no protests and so Jonathan, shaking his head in disbelief, returned to his goal-line. Once again the kick was to be taken by Ellel's captain. 'Go on, son,' the team's manager urged. 'You can do it this time. Hit it with everything you've got!'

The question in everyone's mind, of course, was where he'd aim for: would he go for the same spot as last time or look for a new target? The boy himself was in some doubt until he ran towards the ball: and then he decided he couldn't be so unlucky a second time. But it wasn't bad luck that kept the ball out of the net, it was the brilliance of Jonathan's full-length dive. He had gambled on the shot going in the same direction and his reward was not only to save his side from going two goals down, but to inspire them to play their best football of the season in the remaining minutes of the game.

Any team that fails to score from two penalties is bound to be dispirited and for the next couple of minutes Thistle resembled a boxer who'd taken a near-knock-out punch and couldn't remember how to get back to his own corner when the bell went.

Damian, convinced now that fate was wearing a green shirt and yellow shorts, set the example of renewed endeavour when he kept possession after picking up a misplaced pass. Evading a couple of ill-timed tackles, he headed for the right wing, always one of his favourite ploys. Ian, of course, was expecting a pass; but Damian was simply using him as a decoy. The Ellel defence, now riddled with uncertainty, either backed away or just stood-off. Damian made as if to accelerate – and instead hit a crossfield pass with all the strength he could command.

Warren, at that moment in complete isolation, moved to meet the ball as if he'd known it was going to be sent to him even before Damian released it. Pulling it down with his usual economy of effort he took it, equally effortlessly, past the one defender stationed on the route to goal. Like Jonathan, minutes before him, the Ellel goalkeeper knew he had to come out to narrow the angle of any shot. But that was simply his undoing as Warren, with rare accuracy and stunning skill, used his left foot to send the ball looping over the goalie's head and into the net.

'Oh, great goal, GREAT goal!' Damian said, over and over again, as he hugged the scorer.

'No, great pass from you, skipper,' Warren replied, still as cool as ever in spite of all the acclaim he was receiving from team-mates and spectators alike.

It was the sort of goal that ought to have won a match; but it didn't. In spite of Darton's almost incessant attacks until the final whistle, Ellel didn't concede another score. They were a resilient unit and they displayed all the considerable defensive qualities that had helped them to the top of the division. But it was an epic struggle because several times United were within centimetres of putting the ball in the net.

'Well, I reckon that's as good as a win for United – drawing away with the top team,' Damian said to Warren as they shook hands with various opponents. 'But now I really fancy our chances of beating them hollow when we get them back at our place.'

Warren was nodding his agreement when Alex came dashing up with a piece of startling news. 'Hey, you see that chap talking to Jonathan? Well he's a selector for the area football association and he wants to know if Jonathan's interested in a trial for the Redbourne Boys' team! Oh yes, and he wants to see Hajinder in action again, too, because he thinks he's a pretty good goalie as well. Fantastic!'

At that moment they saw Jonathan shake hands with the man and then he came running towards them,his eyes alight with pleasure. They all congratulated him but none could suppress a pang of envy.

'Lucky for me I went back in goal when I did,' Jonathan chortled. 'Just at the right moment to be spotted as a future star!'

'Is it only goalkeepers he's looking for?' Warren asked.

'Shouldn't think so,' Jonathan replied. 'He said he wanted the strongest squad he could find. So he's definitely coming to see our next couple of matches. You three will have to shine then, won't you?'

'Oh, we will,' said Damian fervently. 'We will!'

Also by Michael Hardcastle

IN THE NET

'As the ball bounced gently on the turf, Gary Ansell trapped it under his studs. Quickly he rolled it forward with the side of his boot. No one was in a position for a pass.'

Soccer is the most important thing in Gary's life and though rugby is the game at his new school, it takes more than the influence of a headmaster to discourage him – especially when he's asked to play for Bank Vale United.

The first exciting football adventure about the superstars of the Junior League.

Michael Hardcastle

UNITED!

'Albion can buy players when they need them. And that's what we've got to do, Keith.'

Kevin Ripley's suggestion staggers the boys – but Bank Vale United have to start winning or they stand no chance of getting the Championship. But buying a player from another team causes them more trouble than they anticipated . . .

The second exciting football adventure about the superstars of the Junior League.

A Selected List of Fiction from Mammoth

While every effort is made to keep prices low, it is sometimes necessary to increase prices at short notice. Mandarin Paperbacks reserves the right to show new retail prices on covers which may differ from those previously advertised in the text or elsewhere.

The prices shown below were correct at the time of going to press.

	ISBN	Title	Author	Price
☐	7497 0978 2	**Trial of Anna Cotman**	Vivien Alcock	£2.50
☐	7497 0712 7	**Under the Enchanter**	Nina Beachcroft	£2.50
☐	7497 0106 4	**Rescuing Gloria**	Gillian Cross	£2.50
☐	7497 0035 1	**The Animals of Farthing Wood**	Colin Dann	£3.50
☐	7497 0613 9	**The Cuckoo Plant**	Adam Ford	£3.50
☐	7497 0443 8	**Fast From the Gate**	Michael Hardcastle	£1.99
☐	7497 0136 6	**I Am David**	Anne Holm	£2.99
☐	7497 0295 8	**First Term**	Mary Hooper	£2.99
☐	7497 0033 5	**Lives of Christopher Chant**	Diana Wynne Jones	£2.99
☐	7497 0601 5	**The Revenge of Samuel Stokes**	Penelope Lively	£2.99
☐	7497 0344 X	**The Haunting**	Margaret Mahy	£2.99
☐	7497 0537 X	**Why The Whales Came**	Michael Morpurgo	£2.99
☐	7497 0831 X	**The Snow Spider**	Jenny Nimmo	£2.99
☐	7497 0992 8	**My Friend Flicka**	Mary O'Hara	£2.99
☐	7497 0525 6	**The Message**	Judith O'Neill	£2.99
☐	7497 0410 1	**Space Demons**	Gillian Rubinstein	£2.50
☐	7497 0151 X	**The Flawed Glass**	Ian Strachan	£2.99

All these books are available at your bookshop or newsagent, or can be ordered direct from the publisher. Just tick the titles you want and fill in the form below.

Mandarin Paperbacks, Cash Sales Department, PO Box 11, Falmouth, Cornwall TR10 9EN.

Please send cheque or postal order, no currency, for purchase price quoted and allow the following for postage and packing:

UK including BFPO	£1.00 for the first book, 50p for the second and 30p for each additional book ordered to a maximum charge of £3.00.
Overseas including Eire	£2 for the first book, £1.00 for the second and 50p for each additional book thereafter.

NAME (Block letters) ....

ADDRESS ....

....

☐ I enclose my remittance for ....

☐ I wish to pay by Access/Visa Card Number ☐☐☐☐☐☐☐☐☐☐☐☐☐☐☐☐

Expiry Date ☐☐☐☐